"W

Beth heard the hint of warning in Joel's tone.

Walt clearly imagined himself something of a matchmaker, but the older man couldn't be more wrong. It was obvious that Joel was no more interested in her than she was in him. Tall, dark and paranoid just didn't meet her basic requirements.

But then, no one did—not anymore. How could she ever know whom to trust?

She only had to remember last winter and a betrayal she'd never imagined.

She'd never forgive herself for being so blind.

Dear Reader,

*Lone Star Legacy* is a story that touched my heart. I love exploring issues surrounding difficult family situations, for the road to happiness and fulfillment isn't an easy one for many of us. For Beth Lindstrom, dangers from her past may make it an impossible road to travel. And for ex-cop Joel McAllen, finding the courage to heal old wounds and forge new bonds, after a tragedy in his life, may be the hardest challenge he has ever faced.

I also adore writing about the West. The vast, wide open spaces and incredible beauty of the land have always called to me in an indefinable way, so spending this time in Lone Wolf, Texas, has been a delight. I hope you'll enjoy stopping there for a while, too!

It's such fun to hear from readers. You can visit me at www.roxannerustand.com, where there's a newsletter, plus a monthly contest, articles and information about my upcoming books. If you write me at Roxanne Rustand, Box 2550, Cedar Rapids, Iowa, 52406 and send a SASE, I've got bookmarks and other things to send you.

Wishing you many blessings,

*Roxanne*

# LONE STAR LEGACY
*Roxanne Rustand*

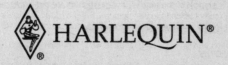

HARLEQUIN®

TORONTO • NEW YORK • LONDON
AMSTERDAM • PARIS • SYDNEY • HAMBURG
STOCKHOLM • ATHENS • TOKYO • MILAN • MADRID
PRAGUE • WARSAW • BUDAPEST • AUCKLAND

ISBN-13: 978-0-373-71442-1
ISBN-10:    0-373-71442-4

LONE STAR LEGACY

## ABOUT THE AUTHOR

**If you could own any horse it would be...** Trigger, from the old Roy Rogers show. He ran faster than the bad guys, knew how to save Roy from all sorts of dangers and his beautiful white mane and tail were always perfectly coiffed. **John Wayne or Gary Cooper?** John Wayne was the image of a strong, taciturn man with unshakable values, who still had a sense of humor. Maybe he wasn't the best actor, but he was one cool cowboy. **Best cowboy name ever?** Grasshopper. He was a real cowboy, too. Years ago we were hauling a yearling to a sale in Kansas. As we were driving through an isolated area with our trailer, a tire broke free and landed in a rocky, rattlesnake-filled ravine. The other tire on that side was also off the axle. We were stranded—no cell phones then—until a cowboy named Grasshopper moseyed by. He looked at the situation and offered us—total strangers—the use of his stock trailer so we could make it to the sale on time. **Cowboys are your weakness because...** there's just something special about a lean, quiet, totally competent man who can be gentle with a horse, sweet to babies and take on anyone and anything that comes his way. **What makes the cowboy?** Definitely the hat—the wrong hat defines a city slicker, and you won't need to look any lower!

### Books by Roxanne Rustand

With many thanks to my husband and children, whose patience and understanding have helped me pursue my dreams. And with ongoing, heartfelt thanks to my dear mom, Arline, who encouraged those dreams from the very beginning.

# CHAPTER ONE

No WONDER the neon-yellow house had stood empty for the past six months. The surprise was that it hadn't been accidentally-on-purpose torched by an appalled neighbor on some dark and moonless night. Situated alone at the far end of Canyon Street, its nearest neighbor was a vet clinic, and no one would have noticed it burn.

But whatever the color scheme or condition, it offered a safe haven and a chance to start over.

Gripping her four-year-old daughter's hand, Beth Lindstrom gingerly stepped past a rusted bicycle, the twisted bumper of an old VW with flat tires, and walked up the dirt path to the front porch. The sign over the door, Crystal Mae's Café—Home-Cooked Food, hung askew.

"Pretty, Momma," Sophie whispered in awe, staring at the fuchsia shutters framing the tall, old-fashioned windows. Her gaze lifted to the high-pitched roof, where a pair of crescent-shaped windows was tucked near the eaves. "And look—it has eyes!"

"Sure looks like it, Poppin. And if I remember

right, the inside is interesting, too." Beth smiled, rmembering just how *interesting* her late Aunt Crystal had been.

A strong, independent Texas woman to the core, she'd turned the main floor of her home into a café after her husband's death. With her ribald sense of humor and good, down-home cooking, she'd made a success of it.

"I gotta *go.*" Sophie looked up at her, clutching her favorite doll. "And Maisie does, too."

"I'm sure you do. It's been quite a while since we stopped." Glancing over her shoulder at her SUV, Beth studied the deserted street, then hit her remote lock button twice and listened for the reassuring, answering honk before turning to fit a key into the front door of the house.

When she'd been here for Crystal's funeral five years ago, the residents of Lone Wolf were comfortable leaving their cars and homes unlocked. Most of them probably still did, but after a lifetime of suburban living, the thought made her shiver... doubly so, after the harassment and accusations she'd faced back in Chicago.

Even though it was all over, the ring of the telephone or a sharp knock on the door still made her flinch.

Despite the cool April days and nights, the café was muggy and smelled of musty decay when they stepped inside. Saying a swift, silent prayer, Beth held her breath and flipped the switches by the front door.

The lights flickered, then bathed the small café in light. Thick dust covered the dozen round tables, most with four chairs, though some of the chairs were tipped over, and several were broken and tossed in a corner. A lunch counter spanned the back wall. Behind it, a faded poster taped to the milk dispenser still read SPECIAL—Eggs, Grits and Beef Hash, $4.95.

Crystal's last special, probably. She'd died with her apron on, and the tenants since then had just rented the upstairs apartment, which had a private entrance. There'd been good renters at first, but then some had to be evicted, according to the Realtor. A few had stolen away in the night, after racking up months of unpaid rent.

"Where's the potty, Momma?"

Jarred back to the present, Beth led her to an open door at the back marked Fillies. She turned on the light and again held her breath...but no mice or roaches scurried away. Thank God.

She quickly wiped the dust from the fixtures with a paper towel, and surreptitiously checked for spiders. "Here you go, sweetie."

Sophie's eyes rounded in alarm. "I don't *like* this place."

"I'll stay right here. I promise."

"But it's *icky.*"

"It's not nearly as bad as some of the gas stations we hit on the way down, right?" Once they'd left the freeways and started across rural Texas, the facilities along the two-lane highways had taken a major turn for the worse, and Sophie had hit her fastidious stage over a year ago. The trip had not been easy.

Pouting, Sophie finally gave in, but jumped back at the rust-orange water that poured from the faucet when she tried to wash her hands. Her eyes filled with tears. "I wanna go *home*."

*Me, too.* But that home was gone forever and this one was going to take its place...at least for a while. Beth swept her daughter up into her arms for a big hug and a kiss. "We're on a great adventure, honey. We're like Dora the Explorer, finding out about new things, seeing new places. It's going to be fun!"

Sophie's lower lip trembled. "Where do we sleep?"

"Upstairs, where my aunt Crystal had her apartment. But..." Beth mentally calculated the cash in her wallet. "We might stay in that little motel on the edge of town, just for tonight, so we can get things cleaned up, first. Okay?"

Sophie nodded, then wrapped her arms tightly around Beth's neck. "I'm scared, Momma."

Beth hugged her back, murmuring gentle reassurances. But that inner voice still whispered through her thoughts, just as it had on the eighteen-hour trip south. *Me, too, Sophie. Me, too.*

JOEL MCALLEN WEARILY STEPPED out of the back door of his Uncle Walt's vet clinic, hefted a circular saw into the back of his crew cab pickup and unbuckled his tool belt. He tossed it onto the front seat and climbed behind the wheel.

Walt appeared at the door of the clinic. "Dinner. Seven o'clock."

"Home. A shower. Bedtime." Joel grinned as he turned the key in the ignition. "You purely wore me out today."

Walt snorted. "Always an excuse, son. Time you got out and partied a little. Maria's made fried chicken, I hear. *And* your favorite pie. Don't show up, and you'll break her heart."

Joel wavered at the image of pure heaven in the guise of Maria's fresh peach pie. Juicy, fragrant, in an incredibly flaky crust no one could ever imitate. The housekeeper had worked for Walt since Joel was a boy, and she definitely knew how to pull his strings. "Pie?"

"Seven o'clock." Walt winked. "You could even bring yourself a date, if you had a mind to."

If Joel didn't, it wouldn't be due to a lack of matchmaking efforts by Walt, his former office secretary and a legion of the clinic's female clients. Maybe there wasn't much else to do in this town of nine hundred—even if their quarry was a guy who had a lot of forgetting to do, and who'd rather be alone.

"I'll think on it," Joe said dryly. "One of these days, you might be surprised."

"And you might be surprised to find that there are some real nice women out there. Down-home girls, not like those city girls of yours back home. One of them just might keep you from turning into a hermit."

Walt's late wife had been the love of his life, and he'd never remarried after she died over thirty years ago. Being childless hadn't stopped him from thinking of substitute grandkids, though, and dreamer that he was, he still considered Joel his best hope.

Joel backed out of his parking space and drove around the building toward the entrance, still shaking his head. He glanced at the property next door, then nearly sideswiped a light pole.

Slamming on his brakes, he backed up. Stared. Then threw the transmission into Park, his blood pressure escalating. *Not again.*

For all his laid-back, good-ole-boy humor, at seventy Walt was showing signs of forgetfulness and he wasn't in the best of health. He didn't need the stress of more troublesome neighbors.

According to Walt, the old Victorian house at the end of the road had once housed a pleasant little café run by a woman who lived on the top floor, but after her death there'd been a few good renters... and recently there'd been several who were pure trouble. One ragtag family littered the yard with trash, junker cars and rusted truck parts. Their insolent kids had run wild, skateboarding through the clinic parking lot.

After they moved out in the dark of night, there'd been the two burly guys who'd stayed just long enough to scam Walt into an investment scheme. They'd probably figured the isolated Victorian was safe from prying eyes of the law, because their subsequent arrest yielded even more: a crude meth lab in the basement.

The place had definitely gone downhill over the past year, and with its weathered condition probably wouldn't attract more than riffraff now. But this time, Joel was here—and he wasn't going to stand by and let trouble start all over again.

He got out of his truck and strode over to the far end of the clinic parking lot. Surveyed the growing jumble of boxes and black garbage bags being lugged out of the back of a trailer hitched to an old SUV. Just as he'd thought, the situation did not bode well. Joel cleared his throat and said, "Excuse me…can I bother you for a minute?"

A slender woman crawled backward out of the trailer, juggling an overflowing box of stuffed animals. She staggered as she took a step to the ground.

Stuffed animals?

Her eyes lit up as she surveyed him head to foot. "Oh, thank you, God!"

Dropping the box into Joel's arms, she dusted off her hands. "You are *exactly* what I was hoping for."

At the incongruity of his grim expectations and her delicate appearance, his planned speech about responsible neighbors dissolved. "I—I am?"

"You bet." She thrust out her hand for a quick shake. "Beth Lindstrom. Just help me get all of this inside."

Bemused, he studied her smudged face and the dark circles under her eyes. She was sure a cute little thing, with that curly blond hair escaping its ponytail and those big blue eyes, but she looked as if she were ready to drop in her tracks—sort of like a soccer mom after a long, hard day.

Then again, she could be the girlfriend or wife of yet another undesirable tenant…and looks could be deceiving at any rate.

"This all needs to go in the front door." When he didn't immediately obey, she tilted her head and studied him for a moment, then smiled gently at him and spoke slower. "Just set it to one side in there, and I'll put it all away later."

"Ma'am—" He cleared his throat, attempting to discuss the situation with the cluttered yard and past problems with renters, but she glanced at her watch and shook her head.

"Please, we'll have to talk later. I've got two hours to get this trailer clear back to Austin or they'll charge for another day." With that, she hopped back in the trailer and started rummaging around. A second later, she reappeared lugging a huge suitcase on wheels. She blew at her bangs and shot an impatient look at him. "Is there a problem?"

She had to be all of five feet and a hundred pounds, and he had to smother a laugh at her take-charge attitude. "None at all. I'll be glad to help, though I think you must be expecting someone else."

Her hand fluttered to her mouth, a rosy blush suffusing her cheeks. "A guy at the gas station said he'd send someone named Hubie. That…isn't you?"

"Afraid not. I'm Joel McAllen." He hiked a thumb toward a building she'd glimpsed through the trees. "I'm remodeling my uncle's vet clinic next door."

She groaned. "So I almost commandeered a total stranger?"

"Easy mistake." He shrugged. "But since your helper isn't here, I can pitch in."

She hesitated, obviously embarrassed, yet her longing glance at the overloaded trailer spoke volumes. "Well…"

"Let's get moving, then." He took the suitcase from her, and shouldered a cardboard box. "This won't take long."

He dutifully hauled box after box into the old Victorian, though why a woman like her was moving into an abandoned café escaped him. Even in her jeans and a plain white top, she definitely had the air of someone who was upper class.

When he settled the last box on the floor he dusted his hands against his Levi's and turned around to find her counting out a number of bills from what appeared to be a meager stash in her wallet.

"Here you are," she said, thrusting out her hand. "As promised."

He waved away her offer. "Just being neighborly. But I do—"

"Please, take it. I would've paid that Hubie fellow…." She earnestly held out the money. "It's the least I can do."

"I'd rather just ask a few questions, if you have a minute."

He must have inadvertently slipped into his old interrogation mode, because her chagrin changed to frank wariness and she took a step back. "What about?"

Though he'd left the department last fall and had no intention of ever going back, years of experience with the Detroit police force instantly ratcheted up his curiosity at her tense expression.

"I see from your plates that you lived in Illinois." He slipped an easy smile into place. "What part?"

"Chicago." She bent over a cardboard box and began ripping back the sealing tape.

"City or suburbs?"

"We…moved around quite a lot."

He whistled. "Quite a change, coming to a small town like Lone Wolf."

"Just a temporary one." She checked her watch.

"Look, I'd love to visit, but I really don't have time. Was there anything else?"

*Temporary?* That was certainly good news. "Do you know the owners of this house?"

Again, that flash of wariness. "Why?"

He hesitated, choosing his words carefully. "The last renters obviously left it in poor shape, and they weren't the best neighbors. My uncle Walt tried to buy it a few months ago, but the Realtor said it wasn't for sale."

"What would he do with it?"

"Bulldoze the buildings, then sell the land or turn it into more parking for the clinic, probably. The place isn't worth much, anyway—and it would solve a lot of problems in the neighborhood."

She bristled. "That's what he thinks?"

"That's the local consensus, and the owners obviously don't care about it. All I need is a way to contact them directly." He winked at her. "If they sell, you'll be able to find a better place to live. I even know where there's some free labor to help you move."

"Actually, the owners do care—very much," she retorted. "My sister and I inherited this property from our aunt, and it's a beautiful house...or was, until recently."

Surprised, he did a double take. "You?"

She stiffened. "And my sister. After the funeral, we had to clean out Crystal's possessions, and we made sure things were in good repair. But Melanie lives in Billings and I lived in Chicago, so we hired a local Realtor to manage the property. As long as there was rental income, we assumed... Well, we obviously misplaced our trust. I figured I'd spend the summer on cosmetic improvements and some minor updating, but seeing it today was quite a shock."

"So why not just get rid of it? Fast and easy sale, and you could be on your way."

"Frankly, it'll be worth a great deal more when I'm done." She stuffed two twenties into his hand. "And then I promise you, it won't be dirt cheap to someone who wants a parking lot."

Something stirred behind the lunch counter. A moment later, a little strawberry blond preschooler rounded the corner, a rag doll clutched at her chest. From her tousled hair and drowsy eyes, she must have been asleep.

"Hi, there," he said, taken by her winsome expression.

Her eyes grew wide and somber as she looked up at him. "You look like my daddy," she whispered sadly. "But he's dead."

Speechless, he stared down at her as a sudden chill made him shiver. *Like my daddy...*

When his heart finally started beating again, he dredged up a ghost of a smile, then turned and walked out before his knees could give way.

He knew the woman was watching him leave

and probably thought he was crazy, but it didn't matter. He'd stopped by with a sense of righteous indignation over the welfare of his uncle, thinking that yet another pack of troublemakers was moving into the house next door.

Instead, he'd been taken aback by its pretty and very determined owner—and apparently had managed to get on her bad side in a matter of minutes. But none of that began to touch the searing pain that ripped through his heart at the little girl's unexpected words.

The strawberry blond hair…the long, silky ringlets…the dusting of freckles across her pert little nose…he'd dreamed a thousand times about just such a child.

On long, sleepless nights, the image had often haunted him until he finally left the house and walked aimlessly through the dark streets of Detroit, half wishing that some carload of cocky young punks would pull over and challenge him with a .44 Magnum…and half wishing that he would lose. In the early days, it might have been a blessed relief to leave his guilt and pain behind.

The child was the image of what he'd always imagined his little girl would've looked like—if she'd lived.

DR. WALT STOOD on the front steps of the clinic and watched Joel's pickup roar out of the driveway and head out into the country.

"Who set that boy's tail afire?" Loraine Gilbert, who'd been in Walt's high school class back in the dark ages and who was one of his longtime clients, stood next to him holding a squirmy black Lab pup in her arms. "You'd swear the devil was after him."

"Maybe he is." Walt tipped his head toward the place next door, where a little girl and her mother were climbing into an SUV hitched to a trailer, both with out-of-state plates.

The young woman appeared to be in her late twenties or early thirties, and she was a hard worker, lugging much of the stuff out of that trailer alone, until Joel stopped over to pitch in. "And maybe it's time he got shook up a little."

Loraine snorted. "I thought you wanted to buy the place and get rid of that mess. Now you're in for another siege."

"Take a good look." He nodded toward the woman next door. "Now who does she remind you of?"

Loraine squinted into the late afternoon sun as the SUV pulled away. "Same red hair."

"Same skinny build."

"Shorter, though. Not so tall and gangly." Loraine shot a quick glance at Walt, as if trying to read his thoughts. "Though I guess you sort of liked 'em that way, back in the day."

The wistful note in her voice caught him by surprise. "Crystal was just a friend. A good friend,

Lorrie. You know I never looked at another woman after my wife passed on."

"You should have, you know." The pup pedaled its paws wildly until she finally put him down. He bounded to the end of his leash but then spun around and barreled back to collide with her jeans. "You would've had a passel of kids, and by now, you'd have a whole herd of grandkids."

"I just didn't have the heart. But Joel here isn't going to make the same mistake."

Loraine harrumphed, though there was now a twinkle in her eye. "I hear it's not going so well just yet."

"Stubborn. That boy is plumb stubborn, but no one can outlast pure temptation—not when Texas grows the prettiest little gals you'd ever hope to see. Like you, for instance." He chuckled at her faint blush, thankful for their years of deep, comfortable friendship. "So what about that granddaughter of yours? She available?"

"Sissy's only seventeen, you old goat. As you well know." She elbowed him in the ribs, then shot a quelling glance at him as she scooped up the puppy and headed out to her truck. "Your nephew is a loner, and he's carrying a load of trouble in that heart of his. He's the last thing any girl needs."

## CHAPTER TWO

"It's a big spider, Momma. Hurry!"

With a rueful shake of her head, Beth set aside her dust mop in the bedroom and followed the sound of Sophie's voice.

It was hard to believe how radically life had changed. Twelve months ago, Beth had chaired a meeting of the Ladies Auxiliary League, with community beautification as the number one topic on the agenda. Afterward, she'd driven her new Escalade home to prepare steaks on the grill for Patrick's boss and his wife. They'd dined out on the deck, where Beth had lit dozens of candles for just the right ambiance.

Given the events between then and now, those days might have been a century ago and on a different planet.

"Where is it, sweetie?"

Sophie pointed upward. "In the wall. I *heard* him."

"Um…I think it's probably another mouse." Though she'd been setting mousetraps and sweeping spiderwebs for two days, there still seemed to be a plentiful supply. And she didn't even want to think about the fire ants that might be outside, lying in wait on that dusty patch of grass in the backyard. "Just don't touch *anything* that moves, okay?"

Sophie nodded solemnly, her doll clutched at her chest, and a fistful of crayons in her other hand. "Do we have to sleep here tonight?"

"Tonight's the night, now that the new mattresses have arrived. It'll be fun."

Well, maybe not fun, but after a gallon of Pine Sol and countless hours of scrubbing, at least it would be clean. Beth turned slowly around and surveyed the upstairs apartment.

It was rather quaint, really, with its fanciful windows and hardwood floors. Just the basics—two bedrooms, a sitting room, a small kitchen and a tiny bathroom. But it seemed oddly bare without Aunt Crystal's endless collections of dolls and curios filling every nook and cranny. And empty, without her raucous laughter and boundless joy over the smallest things.

Sophie settled down at the kitchen table with her coloring books. "Did you come here when you were little?"

As always, Beth turned so Sophie could see her speak. "Maybe once a year. I just loved running up the front and back sets of stairs." She smiled, remembering. "And I loved all the little storage areas tucked away under the eaves. Some of them connect, so my sister and I used to play hide-and-seek."

Sophie looked down at her coloring book and industriously scribbled orange on a page. "I wish I had a big sister."

Saying that maybe she'd have a sister "someday" seemed so far-fetched that Beth couldn't form the reassuring words. After her husband's betrayal, remarriage wasn't something she'd ever contemplate. "I know you do. But we have each other, right? And come fall, you'll meet all sorts of kids at preschool when we finish fixing up this house and move to Billings."

"Where Auntie Melanie lives."

"Right. And she can't wait until we get there. She's already looking for a nice place for us to live—"

The sound of someone knocking at the door echoed throughout the first floor and up the stairs. "Oops, we'd better run down and answer that. Could be the curtains I ordered for us."

"With My Little Pony?"

"My lace curtains and your pretty ones, too."

But the man at the door wasn't from UPS. He was the gray-haired veterinarian from next door, who waved every time he saw her, and had sent his office girl over with a cake yesterday. But friendly waves and treats would not soften her toward a lowball bid on this property, if that was his intent.

"Howdy." He grinned at her and offered his hand as soon as she opened the door. "Walt Sherbourne."

She wavered, then opened the door wide. "Beth Lindstrom."

"Who has to be the spitting image of her…aunt?" He clasped her hand warmly, his broad smile deepening the crinkles at the corners of his bright blue eyes. "Seeing you brings back some good memories."

"Crystal was my aunt, yes." Beth felt some of her tension ease. "You knew her well?"

"She was a good friend of my late wife's, when they were youngsters, and she ran the café for years. She must've had the biggest heart in the county." His eyes took on a faraway expression. "I swear, she could make a statue laugh."

"That was my aunt, all right." Reassured, Beth smiled. "Won't you come in? I'm afraid we're not ready for company, but I'm working on it."

He stepped inside, then surveyed the café with an approving gleam in his eye. "Planning to re-open? This town could sure use a place to eat, and you'd do a good business."

Startled, she shook her head. After talking to his nephew, she'd expected him to disparage her efforts, then casually offer some ridiculously low figure—something she could not afford to consider.

"I'm here to fix up the place, so it can go on the market by August. Then we'll be leaving for Montana."

"Montana?" He appeared taken aback. "Now, why would you want to leave a dandy place like this? Friendly town." He winked. "Nice neighbors."

His words surprised her, but before she could form a reply, little footsteps came running across the floor behind her, then Sophie wrapped her arms around Beth's waist.

Walt pursed his lips, his eyes twinkling. "You know, I thought I saw a bunny come hopping across the room—but it disappeared."

Sophie giggled and peered around Beth's side.

"Well, look at this—it's not a bunny." Walt rocked back on his heels. "It's a *girl!*"

Sophie came out a little farther.

"And a right pretty one, besides." He smiled down at her, then shifted his attention back to Beth. "I'm sorry I didn't get over sooner to say howdy. My office manager went off and got married last weekend and left me high and dry, so things are a mite wild over at the clinic."

*Here it comes.* He'll assume I'm completely naïve, and…

"First, I want to loan you a cat."

She felt her mouth drop open.

"A cat," he repeated. "I know how these older houses are, and this place has been empty for quite a while. Figured you could use a good mouser, so I brought you a loaner." He retrieved a small cage from the front steps. "Unless you have allergies or a strong aversion to cats, Darwin is your man."

*Darwin?*

Sophie squealed with delight when he put the cage on the floor. "Black-and-white spots! He's so pretty, Momma!"

"Yes, indeed," she said faintly, oddly touched by the unusual favor. "That's nice of you. But I don't have litter, or a box, or food…"

"I've got all that next door in the clinic. Figured I wouldn't haul it over until I knew you wanted help."

Beth closed her eyes and thought of all the traps she'd set without catching a single mouse. "We do. Oh, my—do we ever."

Walt glanced fondly at the cage. "He's sort of the clinic mascot. He's had all of his vaccinations, of course, and he's declawed and fixed. So don't let him outside. If you want to give him back, just say the word. I'll take him back in a minute."

"This is so nice of you."

"The other thing is that my housekeeper has wanted to welcome your family to town. Maria thought about bringing over a basket, but she— and I—wondered if you might like to get out of here for a little while, and join us for supper on Saturday night."

"Well, I—"

"The house is just on the other side of town—

105 San Angelo. There might even be a batch of puppies to play with, if any young ladies are interested." With that gentle grin and shock of pale silver hair, he reminded her of a kindly Santa Claus who'd managed to lose his belly. "And just so you know I'm not some crazy old coot—you can talk to the sheriff, or you can ask about me down at the bank."

"I'm sure I don't need to worry. But I have so much to do...."

"Please, can we go?" Sophie tugged on her sleeve. "Puppies! *Please?*"

Feeling as if she'd just been expertly outmaneuvered, Beth laughed. "I guess we'd better."

A simple dinner. A nice old man who'd been a friend of her aunt's. Puppies. It all sounded like a pleasant break from the endless cleaning and growing list of expensive repairs that would need to be hired out—if she could come up with enough money. So why did she have this odd premonition that Walt Sherbourne had something up his sleeve?

Before setting foot in his house, she would definitely be checking him out with some people around town, just to make sure it was safe.

*Safe.*

A chill slid through her. It was a word that meant a lot more to her now, after the fear and worry of the past six months. But here, she and Sophie would have a fresh start, far away from the troubles that had dogged them in Chicago. Luckily, that was all over, and who would ever bother to follow them to tiny Lone Wolf, Texas, anyway?

No one. Absolutely no one at all.

"I HAVE NO IDEA how you can find anything in this mess." Joel shook his head, looking at the piles of papers on the receptionist's desk. "You're sure it's here?"

"To the right, by the phone," Walt called out from the back room, where he was castrating an Australian shepherd. "Blue paper."

Slips of paper fluttered to the floor while Joel searched that stack, then the amorphous pile in the center of the desk. "Nothing. How come you didn't hire a replacement when Elena told you she was leaving?"

Long silence.

"Walt?"

Concerned, Joel hurried down the hall. He found Walt standing beside the surgery table, his palms braced on the stainless steel surface and his head bowed. The dog in front of him was still out like a light. "Are you okay?"

Walt lifted his head and gave Joel a tired smile. "Fine. Just…thinking."

"You know this is too much for you."

Walt shrugged as he reached over to turn off the gas on the anesthesia machine, then finished up a few more stitches. "I've got another vet starting in December, and your cousin Liza will be done with vet school next spring. I'll be able to slow down, then."

"If you make it that long. What about office help? A vet tech?"

"You find one who'll come out to this town, and she's got a job. Want to help me move this guy to the floor? You take the hips—easy, now."

They gently positioned the dog on a soft bed of blankets.

"What about hiring some high school girl? Someone who loves animals." Joel studied the sleeping dog. "Someone who can lift fifty pounds of dead weight and not suffer the next day."

Walt's eyes gleamed. "Sorry, maybe I should have moved him myself."

"I'm talking about *you*. Next thing you know, you'll be in traction."

Walt stared up at the ceiling. "I've advertised. I've asked around. Town this size, the labor pool is more like a puddle, and half the people I could think of were ones I wouldn't trust with my animals or my books. But there is someone…she's new around here, and she looks like she could use a job. Got a little girl to feed."

"Not the new neighbor."

"Why not? Looks like she's a hard worker." The dog twitched. Coughed. Walt bent down to remove the trach tube, then he straightened and watched as the dog started to wake up. "Lord knows, fixing up that place of hers will cost a fortune, and I'm guessing she doesn't have a lot to work with."

"Why do you say that?"

"Pretty little thing like her can't do it all, but she sure hasn't hired anyone to help her out. And that SUV of hers looks like it's about to breathe its last. Sounds like it, too."

Walt was right—she was definitely pretty, and Joel had found himself thinking about her way too often since he'd helped her move in. But he'd picked up on some bad vibes—and after fifteen years in law enforcement, he'd learned to listen to them. When he said he'd like to ask her a few questions, she'd gotten skittish. Wary.

It was nothing he could put his finger on, exactly, but until he knew more about her, she wasn't someone who ought to get her hands on Walt's books. It was sheer common sense.

"I think you should hold off a while. What do we know about her? Nothing."

"Her aunt was Crystal Mae, and that's enough for me."

"Right. But even serial killers have normal people in their family tree."

Walt snorted. "That's what you think of that sweet little gal? That she's a *serial* killer?"

"Of course not. But you need to be cautious. Remember telling me about how your dentist lost nearly everything to that accounting firm?"

"I hardly think—"

"And Beth plans to leave town in a few months, at any rate." Joel thought fast. "Think of all you'd have to teach her. And," he added after a deep breath, "I'd guess she needs time to work on that place of hers and get it done."

Walt laughed. "Whale of a lot of protest, over a gal you don't know."

"Consider it professional advice. Steer clear."

"Evil isn't hiding behind every shadow, Joel," Walt murmured as he started writing in the dog's medical chart. "Maybe you worked at that detective job of yours too long."

Okay, so maybe he *was* just a tad cynical. Burned out. He'd been through hell in more ways than one back in Detroit, and he wouldn't even be in this town if that weren't the case.

Beth Lindstrom might be the most honest person on the planet, but she'd seemed oddly edgy, and Walt was far too trusting. That recent asphalt scam wasn't the only time he'd been taken in the last couple years. With just one crafty, light-fingered employee, everything he'd ever worked for could go up in smoke.

Joel was going to make sure that didn't happen.

# CHAPTER THREE

AFTER SPENDING the day with a calculator, a legal pad and two local contractors, Beth felt too overwhelmed to even think straight.

The house had termites, black mold starting in the café storeroom, and a cracked foundation, for starters—nothing unusual in this part of Texas—but together they represented more money than she'd been able to salvage from selling her heavily mortgaged home in Illinois.

And that didn't begin to touch the cosmetic projects that would enhance the café's curb appeal for future buyers.

Once the walls were patched, the house would have to be painted, inside and out. The deeply scarred oak floors needed stripping. Several windows and doors had to be replaced, and if the stains on the upstairs bedroom ceilings were any clue, the roof had serious problems, too.

And the plumbing—she closed her eyes, trying not to remember the plumber's look of shock that soon brightened to an avaricious gleam as he'd studied the antiquated pipes. A new water softener and iron filter alone would be over five hundred.

Her sister, Melanie, on yet another marriage and perpetually broke, had given Crystal's property little thought since they'd received the inheritance five years ago. Beth had been equally guilty, caught up in her own world, and they'd let a careless Realtor manage both the upkeep and the rentals. No wonder the house had attracted just low-end types.

After Beth recouped her expenses, she and her sister planned to split the remaining profits. Beth had hoped her share would provide a significant down payment on a decent place to live in Billings, but that dream had faded with the last contractor. The cost of bringing this place up to code for a buyer's mortgage inspection would probably approach or even exceed its market value.

She could do a lot of cosmetic work herself, but it still would have to be sold as a fixer-upper for a ridiculously low figure. Maybe Joel had been right about bulldozing the place and simply giving up. Unless…

Her heart picked up a faster beat as she took another hard look at the main floor, then walked into the kitchen, where she found Darwin on top of the old refrigerator, a foreleg, rear leg and his tail dangling down the front surface. He gave her a bored look and went back to sleep.

She studied the possibilities in the kitchen. Her excitement rose. Then dissolved.

Walt had mentioned opening the café again, and he'd said there wasn't any competition for thirty or forty miles in any direction. Reopening the café would create income, and would increase its value to prospective buyers. But to open, she'd have to meet an entirely different set of codes, and that would take money she didn't have, either.

"When can we go see the puppies?"

Sophie had been asking all day. "I don't think…" Beth looked at the clock, wanting nothing more than to cancel that dinner invitation. But one glance at her child's hopeful expression and she just couldn't do it.

After seeing her entire life tipped upside down, Sophie had still taken everything in stride—leaving her pretty pink bedroom, the kids next door, the only house she'd ever known. And this was really such a small thing. What was the harm?

She managed a weary smile. "Guess we'd better get dressed and get over there. Can't keep those pups waiting, right?"

AFTER A LONG, hot shower, Beth gave Sophie a bath and then lingered over her own closet, uncertain over what to wear. Until now there'd been no question—her worst jeans and shirts, because she'd been endlessly cleaning and scrubbing, and today, she'd started clearing out some of the rubbish in the yard.

But for an evening? Sophie immediately chose her favorite purple Dora dress, but most of Beth's wardrobe was in storage back home. She finally grabbed cream slacks and a peach knit top, added gold hoops and a bracelet, then twisted her hair up in a loose bun.

Walt's friendly greeting and his housekeeper's welcoming smile made her thankful that she'd taken those few extra minutes to look nice. "You have a lovely home," she murmured.

And it was. Most of the houses in town were single story with wood siding, and nearly all of them had deep, open porches to shade against the blistering Texas sun.

Walt's home was a two-story brick, spacious and inviting, but with no pretensions of grandeur. Every bit of woodwork and furniture glowed softly from Maria's loving care, and a mouth-watering aroma of some sort of Mexican entrée filled the air.

"Are the puppies here?" Sophie said eagerly. She tugged on Beth's hand. "Can I see them?"

Walt laughed. "You bet. They can't wait to see you, either." He led the way through the living and dining rooms, then down a hallway leading to the kitchen and back door.

When he ushered them through the door to the

screened porch, a litter of yellow-and-black lab pups tumbled out of their blanket-lined box.

Their mother, a gleaming black lab, lifted her head to check out the newcomers, then flopped back down, clearly exhausted by her rambunctious family.

Sophie squealed with delight when the pups swarmed around her, licking her fingers and crying to be picked up.

"The screen door is locked and ole Shadow is a good watchdog," Walt said. "So your daughter should be okay, if you'd like to come inside for a drink?"

"Just tea or lemonade, if you've got it." She inclined her head toward Sophie. "I think I'd better stay close by in case she gets overwhelmed."

Walt called out to Maria, and she returned a few moments later with a tray of lemonade, tortilla chips and homemade salsa that she set on a glass-topped wicker table.

"Dinner will be in ten minutes." She shot a questioning look at Walt. "Okay?"

Walt glanced at his watch. "Perfect timing." He settled into one of the four white wicker chairs at the table and waved Beth toward the one across from him.

The chairs sported bright cushions that echoed the massive pots of red geraniums on the porch steps. Graceful ferns hung from the porch ceiling, and at one end, a long, low table was filled with colorful Mexican pottery bearing a variety of plants.

"This is so pretty. I hadn't realized just how nice it would be to get away for an evening," Beth said. "And Sophie is thrilled, as you can see."

The puppies scrambled over each other, whining and vying for attention when Sophie sat down, though a couple toddled back to their nest.

Walt smiled. "We don't have the pleasure of young folks here very often, and that's the best part of having pups. What do you think, Sophie? Aren't they fun?"

She ignored him, and Walt gave Beth a curious look.

"She can't hear you," Beth said quietly. "She's facing the other way, and the puppies are noisy."

"Bless her heart." Walt's voice was filled with compassion.

"She had partial hearing loss after an accident, but she's slowly improving. She manages pretty well if someone speaks up, and does best when she can watch your lips and expression."

"My brother Gerald was hard of hearing. Though for him, it was sort of selective," Walt added with a twinkle in his eye. "The man never missed hearing an invitation to dinner."

Walt's gentle humor reminded her of her late grandfather, and for the first time in weeks, Beth felt herself relax. "I'm so glad you invited us over tonight."

"How is Darwin working out for you?"

"He's quite a mouser." Beth shuddered. "I hate to tell you how successful he's been, though I'd swear he never leaves the top of the refrigerator, and does nothing but sleep. He lined up his prizes on the floor by my bed this morning. So far, he's massacred six."

"He's just showing off." Walt took a sip of his iced tea, set it aside, then braced his elbows on the arms of his chair and steepled his fingers. "How's everything else going?"

She felt her smile waver. "Fine. Working hard."

He gazed at her thoughtfully. "It's expensive, doing everything up right. I imagine that house will need a lot of work. More than just a paintbrush and scrub bucket, at any rate."

"True." Disappointment flooded through her as she realized that this dinner invitation was probably nothing more than a sociable way to make a bottom-dollar offer on her place. One she couldn't afford to accept, because she still had hopes that it would be worth a little more after she'd spruced it up.

"I have a little proposition for you."

Here it comes. She sipped her lemonade. "What is it?"

The screen door to the house swung open, and Joel stepped out into the porch. His face registered surprise when his gaze landed on Beth. Surprise that quickly faded to a hint of exasperation. *"Walt."*

"Did I forget to tell you about our other guests? You've met, I believe."

Joel spared Beth a brief nod of acknowledgment, then pulled up a chair and sat at the table. "What's this about a proposition?"

"I know what I'm doing," the older man said mildly.

"I think we should talk a bit first, don't you?" A muscle ticked on the side of Joel's lean jaw.

He'd recently showered, and his dark hair was still damp and swept back. She'd caught the scents of soap and a faint touch of Stetson aftershave when he passed by, and in those khaki slacks, loafers and a black polo shirt that molded to his broad chest, he could have been some urban guy heading out for an evening in the city.

A dark and handsome one, at that—all lean, tanned angles and planes, and a flash of white, perfect teeth when he smiled. Which, come to think of it, he'd managed just once since she'd met him. There was a world-weary depth to his compelling, whiskey-brown eyes that suggested he'd seen the worst life had to offer and rarely found a reason to smile.

"I think this young lady would be a real asset," Walt said. "And God knows things at the clinic are getting worse by the day."

"The clinic?" She raised her hands in protest. Good grief—were they talking about *hiring* her? "Hey, I really don't—"

"You'd have to fill out an application, of course." Joel leaned back in his chair and angled his attention toward her. "With references. Do you have any work experience?"

"I—was catering manager at a hotel, until I had Sophie. And then I stayed at home."

"Why did you move to Texas?"

"I think we've discussed that already." Anger flared deep in her belly at his subtly confrontational air. "I didn't come here looking for a job, so maybe it's time for Sophie and me to leave."

"Hold on, hold on." Walt shook his head and motioned them both to settle down. He directed a benevolent smile at Beth. "Please, forgive us. Maria and I truly did look forward to having you over."

She wavered, wishing she'd never come.

"But then I also started thinking that you might be interested in a short-term job," Walt continued. "Just until I can find someone permanent. And," he added with a nod at Sophie, "I'll bet Maria could even help you find some good child care."

Joel cleared his throat and fixed Walt with a stern look.

"For Pete's sake, Joel. Lighten up." Walt waved a hand at him in dismissal. "I'm sure a few references would be no big deal."

Beth looked over and found Joel's gaze riveted on her face. She had the uneasy feeling that he was picking up on her thoughts, examining them and judging her.

Suddenly determined to stay, if only to defy him,

she gave Joel a bored glance and turned to face her host. "Since we're all getting to know each other so well, I'm curious about your nephew. He certainly isn't very friendly, for a small-town guy."

Walt chuckled. "He's pretty new to these parts, too. What—going on six months, Joel? He bought some livestock and a ranch way out in the country. I hardly ever saw him until he started remodeling the clinic. Holed himself up out there, thinking he could just—"

*"Walt."* There was a hint of warning in Joel's voice.

The older man scooped up some salsa with a tortilla chip and waved it at her, grinning. "Guess he'll just have to tell you himself. Maybe you two can get together."

"I'm sure it's a fascinating tale. Maybe another time." She left the table to sit on the floor with Sophie and the puppies until Maria came to call them in to dinner.

Walt clearly imagined himself something of a matchmaker, but he couldn't be more wrong. It was obvious that Joel wasn't interested, and she sure wasn't. Tall, dark and paranoid just didn't meet her basic standards.

But then, no one did—not anymore. How could she ever know whom to trust?

She only had to remember the accident last winter, and a betrayal she'd never imagined. She'd never forgive herself for being so blind.

JOEL SETTLED BACK with one elbow propped on the arm of his chair, his coffee cup in one hand. As always, Maria's tamales and enchiladas had been incomparable, while the rich, creamy caramelized flan and fluffy sopaipillas were the perfect, sweet balance to her strong coffee.

But the conversation around the table couldn't have been more awkward.

Between the glowering looks Walt shot at him and the tension radiating from the woman across the table, Joel figured this would be a three-Rolaids night for everyone except the little girl, who seemed blissfully unaware of the emotions swirling above her head.

After seeing Sophie the first time, he'd gone home, tossed back too much Scotch, then lost himself in his own grim memories. The hangover and his strength of will had helped shove those images back into some dim recess of his brain, and he'd vowed that he wouldn't let them surface again.

But now, looking at the little girl's sparkling eyes and listening to her childish chatter about puppies and cats and some friend from back home named Lizzie, his melancholy resettled over him like a suffocating cloud. He wanted nothing more than a quick escape.

"…so what do you think?" Walt lifted his coffee cup toward Beth in salute. "Want the job?"

Joel jerked his thoughts back to the present. "I

thought we—you—were going to do the usual reference check, and all that."

Walt ignored him. "Well?"

Beth shot a defiant glance at Joel. "I'd be glad to give it a try."

Joel exhaled slowly, considering. His caution was probably misplaced, but as a cop, he'd seen more than his share of con artists who were experts at charming the socks off easy marks, and it didn't pay to be careless. On the bright side, he'd be working at the clinic, too, and could keep an eye on her for a while. In fact…

"You know what, I was just thinking." He bared his teeth in what he hoped came across as a friendly smile. "I'm looking for more construction work. I could come over Monday morning and shoot you an estimate on your remodeling projects."

Definite alarm flared in her eyes. "I…think I'm pretty well covered already."

"How far out are those contractors booked?"

"A—a month or so." She set her jaw. "Which will work just fine."

"That's a long time to wait," he said mildly. "And you know those dates are probably very optimistic, in order to snag your business. At least let me take a look."

"I don't think so. She glanced at Walt, who gave her an encouraging smile. "It would probably be a waste of your time."

"He does mighty fine work," Walt said. "Just look at what he's done so far in the clinic. But of course, I'm probably biased."

"I..." She wavered, biting her lower lip. Then her shoulders sagged, and Joel knew she felt trapped by common courtesy to her host—and new boss—to at least let his nephew look at the project. "I...suppose another estimate wouldn't hurt," she said after a long pause, her voice noticeably devoid of enthusiasm.

She clearly didn't want anything to do with him, and Joel could hardly blame her for that.

So he was going to make an offer she couldn't refuse.

# CHAPTER FOUR

"ARE YOU SURE?" Beth looked down at the paper in her hand with a dubious expression, apparently adding up the numbers a second time. "This is way below the other estimates."

Joel shrugged. "Seemed fair enough to me."

"B-but the materials. Your time." She looked up at him and frowned. "Have you actually *done* much remodeling?"

"You can check out what I've been doing over at the clinic. I also worked my way through college on a construction crew."

Joel watched her expressive face as she sorted out what was, in truth, an estimate far below the going rate. He didn't need the money right now— he'd only started the remodeling work for Walt to fill his time with something worthwhile, though if he stayed in Texas, he might turn it into a business.

But in this case, he'd wanted to make doubly sure that the client would accept.

The irony was that perhaps he'd gone too low.

"Honestly, I hadn't intended to even consider you, but this estimate is just too affordable for me to pass up," she said slowly. "I know you're still working on the clinic, though, and that should come first."

He nodded. Either way, she wouldn't be far out of sight.

"So how about this—quote me an hourly rate for your labor if I go pick up the materials myself."

He suppressed a grin, and again he shot her a low quote—one that barely topped the wage of a convenience store clerk in Dallas.

"Let's go one project at a time, then," she murmured. "If that's okay with you, then I guess we have a deal."

"So…where do you want to start?"

She led the way from the café into the dark and dingy kitchen. "Once I can get the café up and running, it will help finance the rest of the work, and might also make this place more desirable to buyers.

"I'll do the painting." She tapped her copy of Joel's estimate. "But all of those old wooden butcher-block counters have got to go. The floor tile needs to be replaced. The vent system is filthy, to say the least. The three-compartment sink leaks. With this low estimate of yours, I'll be able to afford a small commercial dishwasher, but it will need to be installed."

"Not a problem. So tell me," he added casually,

"why are you tackling this whole place on your own? No steady guy around to pitch in?"

"I…" She turned away and picked up an old teapot. Studied the label underneath. "You probably heard my daughter mention her father, on that first day."

He nodded.

"He died about a year ago. Unexpectedly—in a single car accident." She unconsciously touched a thin white scar tracing the edge of her cheek and temple. "Sophie and I were with him." Her mouth curved into a faint, sad smile. "She was just three, and now she thinks every tall, dark-haired man looks like her daddy."

Sophie was napping now, thank God, but at just the mention of her name, painful images from the past blindsided him. She was so sweet, so innocent. So very, very fragile.

And in the space of minutes, a precious child could be gone forever. It was a responsibility he never wanted to face again.

"Joel?" Beth was staring at him, the wariness back in her eyes.

He jerked his thoughts back into the present and scrambled for a response. "I—I'm sorry about your loss."

"We're doing okay. It's harder for Sophie, because she suffered some hearing loss and she still has nightmares." She stared over his shoulder, her brow furrowed. "I've tried and tried to remember what happened, but it's all a total blank from the time we left home until I woke up in the ICU sometime the next day."

Some of his perceptions about Beth shifted.

Of course anyone who'd been through such a tragedy would be deeply affected. Her wariness was probably a perfectly normal reaction by a grieving, vulnerable widow alone in a strange town.

"Perhaps that's for the best." He suddenly felt awkward, out of his depth. "Not remembering the accident, that is."

"No." Her knuckles whitened around the spout of the old china pot. "Sometimes Sophie wakes up screaming, saying things that make no sense. If I could remember, maybe I could help her."

She winced, then opened her hand and looked down at her palm. The spout lay there broken, and blood welled from a cut at the base of her thumb. "All I can do is hold her, and tell her that everything will be all right. But that's no help at all."

BY THE END OF THE WEEK, Beth knew two things— that she'd never make it as receptionist/bookkeeper, and that no project was ever as easy as it looked.

"Tell me again about Elena," she grumbled at Walt as he passed by the front office with a Schnauzer tucked under his arm. "She was a paragon, right?"

"She was."

It was always interesting to hear Walt's views

about his former employee while trying to make sense of Elena's innovative filing system. "Um…doesn't *P* usually come after *L,* or is it just my imagination?"

He backed up and peered over her shoulder. "That's the Petersons' file. They have llamas."

"But it's under *L.* She filed under types of *animals?*"

He smiled patiently at her. "Now, that surely would be too confusing for a ranch, wouldn't it?"

Beth bit back a growl of frustration. "Yes, it surely would. But you say Elena got married, and she won't be back. Is that correct?"

"Afraid so." He shook his head sadly and moved on down the hall.

"Then I've got a month or so to fix this filing system before some other poor soul has to deal with it," Beth muttered under her breath. "Unless I go mad before then."

Joel walked in the front door with his tool belt slung low on his hips and an armload of two-by-fours. He lifted an eyebrow, apparently picking up on her frustration. "How's the job?"

"The animals are great, and that's as far as I'm going. Except for Walt, of course." She paused, considering. "And I guess you aren't as grumpy as I first thought."

He laughed. "Admit it. You'll miss this place when you open that café of yours."

"Not the filing system." She smiled back at him,

relieved at the easier camaraderie they'd gradually developed over the last four days.

He probably just felt sorry for her, what with the loss of her husband and the all-too-visible scars she tried to hide with a loose hairstyle and long-sleeved shirts. But as much as she disliked pity, it was better than his sharp-eyed suspicion from the week before.

She truly did enjoy being here at the clinic for a few hours at the end of every day, and it had to be good for Sophie to spend time with other children at her new babysitter's place, too.

"I'll be stopping by again tonight," Joel said as he passed the desk empty-handed, heading outside for another load. "I can install stainless steel counters for the café from a set I found in an old bar, if you're interested. The owner says you can have them all for fifty bucks."

"That's fantastic." Filled with gratitude, she watched him go out the door, then flopped back in her chair and sighed.

He'd been over nearly every evening, working until midnight. Finding shortcuts and cost-saving materials that were as good or better than she would have paid for new.

In another place, another time, she might just be a little infatuated with him, watching that smooth ripple of muscle play beneath those T-shirts, hearing his deep laugh. Seeing his skill at making something beautiful out of almost nothing. But there were a dozen reasons why that wouldn't happen, and she only had to think about Sophie— whom Joel carefully avoided—or Patrick to bring the biggest ones to mind.

Being a fool once had been bad enough.

Walt strode back down the hall and handed her a slip of paper. "Payday. Every Friday, so you can keep up on things at home."

She accepted it with just a glance at the number, then took a longer look. "This has to be a mistake."

"No mistake. You're saving this place from total ruin, and me from keeling over from stress." He grinned and turned on his heel. "I'm heading for home now. Just forward all the calls to my cell when you leave."

"But really—"

He waved and went out the back door, leaving her to fan herself with the check. Could it be that things would actually work out here?

The café phone had been installed yesterday. It wouldn't be long before she could decorate the little place and then start ordering food supplies.

She smiled, imagining a bakery case of lovely almond crescents. Cream-filled *croque en bouche*. Baguettes. Tempting little salads, artfully arranged, with a golden brioche on a matching plate, and a select variety of teas and coffees to tempt the palate.

How could she go wrong?

THE NEXT DAY, Joel stopped by the front desk and stared over her shoulder at the menu she'd drawn up on the clinic computer during her coffee break.

He was speechless for a moment, then he burst into laughter. "Sugar, do you know where you are? You're in the middle of rural Texas. Home of road-house barbeque, chicken-fried steak and sweet tea. Folks in this town aren't gonna know your fancy teas from a turnip."

Affronted on behalf of all the Texans in…well, Texas, she drew herself up to her full height. "If they haven't tried my kind of menu before, they'll be surprised. And happy."

"They aren't going to be happy. They're gonna be mystified. Now give 'em corn bread and a pot of pinto beans, and they'll know what you're talking about."

"I've been to Dallas. It's a very cosmopolitan place."

"Right. But this is a bitty town two hundred miles from nowhere." He raised his hands, palm up, in a gesture of defeat. "Do what you want. I'm just saying…"

He turned away, but apparently couldn't help himself, because he came right back. His lips twitched. "And another thing, you buy breakfast out here, and it isn't brioche and a latte. It's hot biscuits. Jalapeño roast beef hash or fried ham. Eggs. Fried potatoes. And don't forget the grits and hotcakes. These ranchers want good fuel, not an international experience."

"They're looking for a heart attack."

A teasing glint came into his eye. "Show them your menu, and you'll probably give them a good one."

SOPHIE CUDDLED close to Beth on the couch in their apartment. It was ten o'clock and the poor child should have been asleep over an hour ago, but she'd awakened screaming, with tears streaming down her cheeks.

"I don't want to go to the babysitter. Not anymore."

"I thought you liked Mrs. Garcia. We heard very nice things about her, you know." Beth stroked her daughter's silky hair. "Can you tell me what happened today?"

Sophie sniffled against Beth's shirt. "It's every day."

Beth pulled her onto her lap and held her close. "*What* happened?"

"The k-kids."

"Her kids?"

"Th-the others. They say—" Sophie dissolved into renewed tears. "Th-they say I'm st-stupid."

Beth hugged her tighter and dropped a kiss on the top of her head. "Oh, sweetheart, you know that isn't true. You're the smartest little girl I know."

"They laugh at me!"

Her words were muffled against Beth's shirt, but still cut through her sharp as any knife. "Do you remember what the doctor said?"

"U-use my good ear?"

"He said this was because of the accident, so it has nothing to do with you being smart, sweetie. He said to turn your better ear toward people, and that your hurt ear would get better over time."

"But it *isn't*."

"It has—you're doing so much better already. And in the meanwhile, we just need to make sure people understand that they should talk directly to you." Beth slowly rocked Sophie in her arms, treasuring her warmth. Wishing she could take away every hurt her daughter would ever have. "I'll talk to Mrs. Garcia tomorrow. Then she can tell the kids to speak up."

Sophie pulled away in alarm. "They'll say I'm a tattletale!"

"No, I'll ask her to be really subtle—er, careful—so they won't think that." Beth gently pulled her back into her arms and snuggled her close. "Things will be okay."

Sophie whimpered, but finally her breathing slowed and her little body relaxed into the boneless warmth of sleep. Beth savored her closeness for a few minutes more, then carried her back to bed and tucked her in.

The unfamiliar jangling of the phone—the first time she'd heard it ring—startled her into a fast search for where she'd left the portable receiver.

She nabbed it on the fourth ring from the serving counter in the kitchen. But no one responded when she said hello.

"Crystal's Café," she repeated. "Can I help you?"

"You'd better hope so," the man said on a harsh laugh. As usual, his voice was low and gritty, slightly muffled. As if he purposely lowered its register and was speaking through a heavy cloth over the receiver. "The question is, how fast. It won't be that hard to get to you, if that's what it takes."

She gripped the receiver, her heart hammering against her ribs and her palms sweating. "I—I swear to you, I searched everything. I don't have what you want."

"You owe me, sweetheart, and you'd better think twice, because my patience is wearing thin."

"I…don't have it, and I don't even know who you are. I owe you nothing." She swallowed hard, her fear warring with anger. *It wasn't fair. It wasn't fair.* "You're *crazy.*"

"You don't think the Chicago police would like a little information on you? I figure you're good for fifteen to twenty, federal time."

A familiar wave of dizziness careened through her midsection, leaving nausea in its wake. "Th-there's nothing to tell them, because I did nothing wrong. They didn't press charges of any kind."

"Oh, but they will…when they know more." His voice lowered to a growl laced with pure menace. "Don't make me come after you and that little girl of yours. One way or another, you're gonna give me what I'm after. And believe me, until I get the key and that file, you aren't safe anywhere on this planet—so don't think your little move to Texas was any help at all."

The line went dead.

Beth sagged to the cold floor, the receiver still in her hand, her pulse still pounding in her ears.

From the first anonymous call, she'd desperately started searching for what he wanted, planning to turn it all over to the police—hoping that it would lead to the arrest of the man harassing her.

But there'd been nothing.

No paperwork on any mysterious bank account and no key—though she'd been through every inch of the house in Chicago twice, and had gone through all of her possessions a third time while packing for the move to Texas.

Back in Chicago, she'd reported the man's four threatening calls, but tracing them had led to public phones all over the city. There'd been nothing to go on. Though reporting them had brought the cops back into her life again, and she'd seen the suspicion in their eyes. Then an investigator had shown up at her door—the same one who'd interrogated her after Patrick's death—and his hard-hitting questions had shaken her even more.

What if the caller was telling the truth—and had some sort of evidence that could lead to her arrest? And what would happen to Sophie then?

Wrapping her arms around her knees, Beth closed her eyes and tried to slow her racing heart. There was so much about her husband's secret life that she hadn't known until the police had shown up after his funeral with a thousand questions she couldn't begin to answer.

*Oh, Patrick, what on earth did you do?*

## CHAPTER FIVE

BETH RAPPED SOFTLY on Anna Garcia's front door, then entered when the day-care provider's greeting echoed from somewhere inside.

The usual five-thirty confusion was in progress, with two other moms walking in the door just ahead of Beth to round up their children. A little boy was crying in Anna's arms. Two girls Sophie's age were playing with dolls, but Sophie sat alone with a book and watched them from across the room.

Beth's heart squeezed at her daughter's forlorn expression. Her own time at the clinic flew by, but what were those hours like for Sophie, feeling like an outsider at the age of four? After three days, she still hadn't made any friends.

The taller mom, a slender woman in a pretty mauve sweater and matching skirt, motioned to her daughter, then turned to Beth. "We haven't met yet. I'm Gina Carlton. I'm the principal of the elementary school over in Horseshoe Falls, so these kids will get to know me pretty well in a few years." She nodded toward the other woman. "And this is Tracy Evans."

Beth introduced herself to them both, but Tracy, expensively dressed in matching ivory linen slacks and a cashmere sweater, simply looked over her shoulder and sized Beth up, then turned back to her daughter.

Beth felt a pang at her cool dismissal, so much like the arrogance of her most recent neighbors in suburban Chicago. Two years ago, Patrick had insisted on buying a home in an upscale neighborhood, saying it represented all he'd ever worked for, but she'd never been comfortable with such a high mortgage or in such an affluent area.

Gina smiled warmly. "I understand you're thinking of reopening the café."

"Maybe. It's turning out to be more work than I expected."

"Well, I hope you persevere. Lone Wolf hasn't had a nice place like that in ages. Won't that be great, Tracy?"

The woman in ivory arched one perfect eyebrow. "Bob and I were just talking about it, actually. A lot of folks in town hope the place will be torn down."

Beth drew in a sharp breath. "I'm sorry to hear that."

Tracy shooed her daughter toward the front door. "No offense intended, of course, but there certainly wouldn't be much business in a town like this, and the property is already in ruins. If I were you, I'd save myself the money and the embarrassment."

"Don't listen to her," Gina murmured after the door swung shut. "She and her husband own a restaurant in Horseshoe Falls, and she's been a know-it-all since we were in high school. I think reopening the café would be wonderful for this town. Don't you, Anna?"

The boy in the caregiver's arms had finally stopped whimpering. She gently settled him down next to a stack of wooden puzzles, then walked over to Beth and gave her a quick hug. "Absolutely. I know you plan on leaving at the end of the summer, but we can always hope the new owners will keep it open. And maybe," she added with a twinkle in her eye, "you'll even decide to stay."

Beth glanced between Gina's daughter and Sophie, then chose her words carefully. "I'd love to stay, but we don't have much choice…."

Gina's brow furrowed. "Barely here, then going so soon? This town really wants to keep nice newcomers like you."

"I need a stable job, good enough to support us. Sophie needs a school district large enough to offer special services for preschoolers."

"Special services?"

"She has some hearing loss. It isolates her, because kids her age either ignore her or think she's 'different' and don't accept her."

"I didn't realize." Gina blew out a long sigh. "That has to be tough on her, poor thing."

"She does fine if she can see the face of the person talking and if they speak clearly. Otherwise, she misinterprets certain words."

"What about surgery?"

"The specialist wanted to wait a while. This happened because of an accident, and she's showing gradual improvement. If there's not enough change in six months, we'll need to look at other options...so by then I'll need a job with good benefits."

"But in the meantime..." Gina glanced at Sophie, her eyes filled with sympathy. "You know, maybe my Olivia and Sophie can get together for some play dates. Just the two of them, where it isn't so noisy and distracting. Do you suppose Sophie could come over on Saturday?"

The offer was more than Beth had hoped for. "I know she'd love that."

"It might even help her feel included here, if she has a friend." Gina gave Beth's arm a gentle squeeze, then she dug around in her purse for a business card and handed it over. "This has my cell, home and work numbers on it, so we can figure out the details later."

Scooping her daughter up into her arms, Gina started for the door, then turned back. "Don't even think about what Tracy said. You reopen that café and I promise you'll end up busier than you want to be. I must be related to half the people in this county, and I'll pass the word."

"Thanks!" But Tracy's words kept coming back to her for the rest of the evening. Was it foolish to even think about trying?

"NO, HE'S NOT MARRIED." Following Dorothea Wilbert's intent stare, Beth glanced over her shoulder and saw Joel disappear into Walt's office, where he was installing an entire wall of oak shelving for Walt's library of veterinary books and professional journals. Anticipating the next question, she added, "And far as I know, he is not attached."

"If I was a few years younger..." Dorothea's eyes gleamed. "He's quite a hottie, you know."

"Yes, ma'am." Beth tried to smother a smile, but failed. A *hottie?* The woman had to be eighty if she was a day and her slang was a tad out of date, but she definitely deserved points for sheer spunk.

Dorothea lifted her cat carrier from the counter and angled a look at Beth's bare left hand. "If I were you, I'd snap him right up."

"If I ever decide to start looking, I'll give that some thought," Beth retorted dryly.

At least this was a variation on an all-too-familiar theme. One week at this part-time job, and she'd already fielded questions from at least a dozen women about Joel's marital status. Women who were interested for themselves, or who just happened to have daughters, granddaughters, or nieces who might like an introduction.

Joel tried to avoid them.

Beth found it amusing when he couldn't.

But that interest was no surprise, really. Other than a few grizzled cowhands who'd flirted with her while stopping in at the clinic, she hadn't seen many eligible guys around town.

A situation that suited her perfectly well.

With Walt out in the country on farm calls, the clinic was quiet this afternoon save for a handful of people who'd either stopped in to buy pet supplies, or came to collect their pets after boarding them.

Beth stretched, working out the stiffness in her muscles from last night's siege with a wallpaper steamer, then she turned back to the bank of file drawers behind her.

Joel sauntered up the hall, a carpenter's pencil tucked above one ear, and that gunslinger tool belt riding low on his hips. With a nod in her direction, he went outside.

What was it about him that made her pulse pick up a faster beat whenever he walked by?

He certainly wasn't her type…and she wasn't in the market, at any rate.

In college, she'd gravitated toward the guys with armloads of philosophy books, who talked about the meaning of life, politics or social reform. White-collar guys who were safe, responsible. Who impressed parents and promised the kind of security a smart girl wanted.

Joel had an edge. An air of darkness and danger that promised he could handle any threat that came his way. But she'd learned early on that the bad boys in school were exciting, but they were the ones who casually broke hearts and disappeared. At the age of thirty she'd not be playing that game with Joel or anyone else—especially a man who was so clearly uncomfortable around Sophie.

Luckily, she and Joel had moved past that initial suspicion of his to a fledgling level of friendship, but that was as far as Beth would ever go.

According to Walt, the man had been a cop. A chill swept through her at the thought of what he could uncover if he got a little too curious and began researching her past. What if her anonymous caller was right—and Patrick had somehow tangled her up in the paperwork on his illegal dealings? Or she'd been implicated through some false evidence, by the very person who kept calling her? And then there was that suspicious fire....

She'd been cleared once. But what if the investigators had second thoughts and looked closer?

The clinic door opened and Joel came back in with a box of wood screws and a level. But this time, he didn't just walk on by. He strolled into the receptionist's area and leaned a hip against her desk, his too-long hair disarrayed by the windy day;

his dark, thick lashes and smoldering brown eyes entirely too sexy and compelling.

But it was the hint of a boyish twinkle in those eyes that calmed the nervous flutter in her stomach.

"Ma'am, I need a favor. A big one."

Surprised, she gave him a glance. "If it involves sewing or ironing, you're flat out of luck."

The laugh lines at the corners of his eyes deepened. "What would you say about a date on Saturday night?"

IF HE'D TOLD HER the entire town was afire, she couldn't have paled any faster, though she quickly masked her initial look of shock with a forced laugh. "I...don't think so."

He raised an eyebrow and grinned at her. "Dorothea would say you're making a mistake."

"You *heard* that?" Some color came back into her cheeks.

"Couldn't help it. She has the voice of a revival preacher on Saturday night. Not," he added wryly, "that I believe a thing she said."

"Half the female population of Lone Wolf does, though." She tipped her head and surveyed him from head to foot. "You being a mystery man from the far reaches of the U.S. and all. Most people here probably know each other from birth to death."

"Anonymity is a good thing."

"And speaking of that, I need some facts, so I

know what to say to these people. As in, where you are from exactly, and why you came here." She tapped a forefinger against her lips, thinking. "Oh, and what you did for a living. That's for starters. Unless you just want the local gossips to take care of things."

Joel felt his defenses rise, his muscles tense. "Gossips?"

She gave a delicate shrug. "People know I work here and that you're remodeling the clinic, so they ask me. Walt said you were a cop, but I've heard rumors that you are an ex-CIA agent, an FBI agent, or a private investigator."

He sighed heavily. "Detroit PD. Worked a lot of areas, though the last was homicide. I…just burned out, and needed a change."

He'd made a career of being good at noticing small details. Reading body language. Analyzing behavior and motivation. But even a rookie couldn't have missed the subtle shift of her position, or the brief flare of uneasiness in her eyes.

And he realized that though she'd been superficially friendly, she'd probably been even less forthcoming about her background than him— and was better at blithely skirting subtle questions, too.

"I'm sure it was a tough career," she murmured.

"Challenging. So about Saturday—"

"Mistake. A big mistake." She seemed to cast

around for an excuse, then brightened. "Since we're working together and all."

"There's a *rule?* In Walt's clinic?"

"I'm sure there must be." Her gaze skated away. "Or there should be."

He tried to remember if he'd been turned down with such determination. Probably never, because he and his wife had been high school sweethearts and married young. Later, he'd lost all interest in any sort of social life after the heart-wrenching loss of their daughter, and a subsequent divorce so acrimonious that he still felt singed by Andrea's anger and accusations.

Then he realized that he hadn't quite made his intentions clear. "The town's annual street dance and barbecue is Saturday night. I just thought the evening could be casual—something between friends."

Beth's brittle smile was tinged with disbelief. "You step out on the sidewalk, and I'll bet some gal will swoop by and gladly help you out."

"I am not looking for a relationship, period. The last thing I'd ever do is settle down again, but the local mommas all have hopeful young things looking for a white picket fence and commitment, and they aren't taking 'no' for an answer."

"So, say it louder."

"And disrespect someone's mother? I just figure bringing a date might cool down some of the interest that has come my way."

Her hand fluttered to the thin white scar that traced a faint line from her temple to the corner of her jaw, just below her ear. "I really don't think—"

"Just two acquaintances out for a good time, nothing more than that. Hey, we can talk business the whole time. And the more people see you around town, the more they'll sit up and take notice when you open the café."

"Now that," she retorted with a dry laugh, "is a pretty far reach."

"Whatever it takes." And oddly enough, he realized it was true.

Walt had insisted that Joel meet him for some good Texas barbecue at the festivities, and Joel had figured it might be a good chance to learn a little more about Beth—away from the constant flow of clients in the clinic. But now, he realized just how much he enjoyed her company, and that he really *wanted* her to come along. She was smart, and witty, and—

"I'm not too sure about the dancing part," she said solemnly.

With a start, he remembered the car accident she'd mentioned, and the way she seemed to limp by the end of the day—barely noticeable, but perhaps she tried hard to mask it. "Absolutely."

"And just as fr—" She stumbled over the word. Her gaze skated away. "Colleagues."

He stifled a smile. "Of course."

"And if I can find a good babysitter for Sophie."

"Goes without saying."

If she'd been anyone else on the planet, he might've caved at the reluctance in her voice and let her off the hook. But the more he saw of her, the more she fascinated him on every level.

He wanted to find out what made her tick. Why she was so reticent about her past. Hell, he wanted to tease her into going out on a dance floor, just so he could hold her in his arms and find out if she was as soft and sexy as she looked, because even now she had his dormant hormones slowly coming out of hibernation. "Well?"

Her shoulders sagged. "Then I guess I can help you out."

It was the most lukewarm acceptance he'd ever heard, but it was a start.

SHE'D SPENT THE REST of the day and evening stewing about her foolish decision, but at around midnight Beth glanced at the clock one last time and finally tried to fall asleep by counting and re-counting the reasons that Joel McAllen was a very bad idea.

He was far too handsome for his own good, and she knew just how much a risk that could be. Twice this afternoon she'd found herself daydreaming about behavior entirely inappropriate for a woman widowed just a year.

He was a cop, and that presented an even greater risk.

And with an impressionable young daughter and the tiny apartment the two of them shared, she'd certainly never consider a short-term affair.

Joel was wrong in every way. So why, after saying yes, had she felt her heart lift?

An hour later, Sophie's whimpers awakened her from a troubled sleep. Bleary-eyed, she stumbled into the next bedroom and sat on the edge of Sophie's bed to rest a gentle hand on the child's forehead. "What's wrong, sweetie?"

*"Stop!"* Sophie cried out, clearly still deep in dreams. *"Don't hurt my daddy!"*

It was the same nightmare she'd had a hundred times over during the past year, and it still didn't make any sense.

Beth lifted her daughter into her arms and gently smoothed back the tendrils of hair clinging to Sophie's damp forehead, then rocked her. "It's okay," she whispered. "Mommy's here."

Sophie murmured something and burrowed closer, as if seeking shelter from the demons that still plagued her.

The insurance investigators had said it was an utter miracle that anyone survived the car accident, though Sophie's damage went beyond the physical. Six months of weekly visits with a children's counselor had helped, but hadn't totally eliminated her nightmares about her daddy's blood. The sirens. The pain of her own injuries. Or the unexplainable and unconfirmed presence of a stranger who scared her still.

The counselor suggested that the stranger was a fabrication, a focal point for Sophie's terror over a situation too overwhelming for her to comprehend. The first people on the scene had been a passing highway patrol and then the paramedics, and there hadn't been any threatening strangers according to those eyewitnesses. But fabrication or not, the night terrors were frequent and awful, and Beth's heart twisted at the images Sophie had to face in her dreams.

The phone rang—its harsh tone slicing through the quiet of night.

Beth settled Sophie back under her covers and ran for the phone. *Please, Lord, let this just be a wrong number.*

But even before she picked up the receiver, she knew who it was.

"So you're still there. Chose not to run? That's good to know." The muffled voice was intense, filled with loathing that sent her heart rate into overdrive. He rattled off a post office box address in South Chicago. "Here's your last chance—send what I want, to this address. Priority. No signature required. You've got ten days, or next time, I won't just be bringing matches."

The line went dead.

He'd given her a deadline twice before. Once, he didn't follow through. Several weeks after the second one, there'd been a break-in and a fire at her house.

Shivering she wrapped her arms around her self. *Oh, please, Lord...not again.*

# CHAPTER SIX

JOEL EYED THE REMNANTS of wallpaper festooning the living room of Beth's upstairs apartment and grinned. "Tell me again—how long has this place been in your family?"

"I'm not sure. I think the records showed it was the late 1800s. Why?"

He'd come upstairs to ask her about the placement of shelves in the new cabinets he'd just finished installing downstairs. At his knock, she'd called out for him to come on in, though from the sounds of water splashing and Sophie's giggles, she was busy with bathtime.

"Just curious." He glanced again at the heavily flocked crimson paper. Most of it had been removed, but the remaining tatters seemed to portray buxom women in rather compromising poses.

"Hold on." Sophie's giggles and Beth's laughter floated out into the living room. A few minutes later, the little girl bounced out of the bathroom clad in a purple nightgown with a ruffled hem, her damp hair pulled back in a ponytail and her face pink and glowing.

When he'd first seen Sophie, Joel's heart had wrenched over all he'd lost, and his old guilt and grief had threatened to consume him. Even now, he couldn't look at her strawberry blond hair and sweet little face without imagining what his own daughter would've looked like by now.

Sophie twirled, her arms outstretched, then raced to a basket by the sofa and grabbed an armload of picture books. "Can you read me stories? My daddy did."

He felt the blood leave his face. *My daddy.* "I—"

Beth came around the corner, a towel slung over one shoulder. Her hair was caught up in a ponytail, too, but the steam and the splashing had freed curly tendrils that framed her face, and her damp T-shirt clung to her curves. The look of exhaustion in her eyes turned to sharp awareness when her gaze collided with his. "I'll read to you later, when you're in bed, Sophie."

"But, Mommy—"

"It's time for your bedtime snack, okay? I'm sure Mr. McAllen wants to be going home soon. It's late and he's had a long day." She nodded toward the kitchen table. "I've got cheese, crackers and juice all set."

Sophie's face fell, but she dutifully put the books

back and trudged over to the table and climbed up on a chair.

"I...could have done it," Joel said quietly.

"I just assumed you'd rather not." Beth's smile was bittersweet. "Her dad always said the stories bored him, to tell you the truth. And I've noticed that you don't exactly like being around young kids."

"It's not that." At the look of patent disbelief on Beth's face, he tipped his head toward the basket of books and managed a smile. "It's been a long time since I've read the Fern Hollow books. They were my favorites."

"Really." She studied him for a moment, as if not quite sure of him. "And your most favorite?"

"Definitely Sigmund. For years, I maintained a fantasy about that crocodile coming to my house to eat cream buns."

The disbelief in her eyes faded. "Mine is the one about the seasons. I just love the artwork in that one." She bent to pick up a scattering of doll clothes at her feet. "So, what can I do for you?"

A sudden image flashed through his thoughts that had nothing to do with his work on her café, or children's books, or the bawdy wallpaper on the—

Well, maybe the wallpaper.

She followed his gaze. "Nice, huh? The first layer was pink paisley, and that was bad enough. Under that were layers of purple pansies and 1970s burnt-orange-and-avocado stripes. The red-flocked paper must've been welded on in places, because it sure isn't coming off."

"It's…unusual."

"I don't think you could accuse anyone in this branch of my family with good taste." Her eyes danced. "I'm beginning to think my great-great-grandmother might've run a house of ill repute here. Not that there could be such skeletons in my family tree."

"I'll bet some of the old folks in town would know. You could even play that up in the décor now, if you wanted to do something unique."

"The Bordello—Good Coffee and Fine Food? I'd probably offend half the town if I did that, and I'd confuse the other half. They'd wonder what I had for sale." She braced her hands on her slim hips. "So, how is everything coming with cupboards downst—"

The telephone rang.

Instantly, the color drained from her face.

It rang again. She shot a quick look at the portable receiver on an end table, but made no move to answer it.

"Your phone is ringing," he said gently. "Expecting a call?"

"No…yes." She took an agitated step forward, then halted.

The phone rang again.

"Want me to get that?" When she didn't immediately reply, he sauntered over and picked it up, held it out to her, then hit the talk button when she didn't take it from him. "Crystal's Café."

Walt chuckled. "So you're still there!"

"Working."

"Of course. Never thought otherwise." The smile in his voice was unmistakable. "Hey, could you tell Beth that I need her to come over to the clinic for a few minutes? An emergency came in, and I could use an extra set of hands. I also can't find the Farnsworth file, now that she's straightened everything up. She's welcome to bring Sophie. I'll pay her triple if she can help out."

Joel handed the phone over. "Walt."

He watched the play of emotions on her face. A deep sense of relief, then concern as she eyed Sophie, who was yawning at the table.

"I understand." She listened for moment, then added, "I'll be there" and hung up. "Your uncle says you're good with kids and *totally* trustworthy. Would you mind staying with Sophie for a half hour, so I can go help him? She's so tired that I hate to get her dressed and take her out again."

Time stood still as ice rushed through Joel's veins and terrible memories crashed through his thoughts.

The last time he'd watched his daughter while his wife was running errands.

The absolute, overwhelming panic and fear when he'd gone into the nursery and found his little girl…just a half hour after she'd settled down for a nap.

She'd lain there peacefully, as if sound asleep, soft music still playing on the tape recorder on her dresser.

But with that sweet and terrible lullaby, she'd been ushered from this world into the next. And nothing—not his trembling efforts at CPR, nor the efforts of the EMTs—had succeeded in bringing her back.

If he'd only checked her sooner.

Checked more often.

Stayed in the room with her, watching every breath she took. If he'd done everything right, maybe the world wouldn't have ended for him, as well.

"I—I can't. I'm sorry." He strode to the stairs and descended them two at a time, jogged across the café and let himself out into the cool night air.

He drove like a bat out of hell, disregarding the speed limit on the dangerous curves five miles out of town. Missed the turnoff to his ranch by a half mile. Tires squealing, he did a U-turn in the center of the road.

It wasn't until he pulled to a halt in front of his sprawling ranch-style home that he stopped to consider his actions.

He should have said something—*anything*—before taking off. Beth had needed his help, and he'd cut out on her like some foolish hothead of a teenager.

But he'd been unable to explain his sudden,

razor-sharp sense of panic. The crushing weight of memories that had blindsided him at the thought of staying at her place—alone and responsible—for her little girl. And the worst of it was that his reaction had been totally illogical.

He'd driven as if the devil himself was behind him…yet knew he would never truly escape the past.

So now little Sophie was probably at the clinic in her pj's, curled up on one of those uncomfortable reception area chairs and trying to sleep…and he'd blown off something that might be far more serious than his own troubled history.

The stark look of fear on Beth's face had not been his imagination. She'd been *afraid* to answer that phone. Why?

Setting his jaw, he did a three-point turn and headed back to town at roughly the speed of light.

BETH STEPPED OUT into the cool night air, with Sophie asleep in her arms. Walt stood behind her in the open doorway of the clinic.

"Sure you don't need some help getting home?" he called after her.

"I'm almost there already. But thanks." She crossed the parking lot, sidestepped through the wiry bushes marking the property line and wound through the assorted car parts and litter in her backyard. Glancing over her shoulder when she reached her door, she saw that he was still watching her, like a kindly grandfather making sure all was well.

She waved farewell to him, then shifted Sophie's weight against her shoulder and reached out to unlock the door.

Footsteps crunched on the dry grass, approaching from the side of the house.

*Oh, God.* Biting back a scream, she fumbled with the key. Missed. Tried again, her heart battering against her ribs and her palms slippery with sweat.

A tall figure came around the corner of the back porch. "Beth? It's me—Joel."

Her knees went weak with relief, her fear abruptly turning to anger. "You scared me half to death."

"Your place was still dark, and the lights at the clinic went out when I pulled up in front of your house, so I figured you were on your way home. Here, let me help." He lifted Sophie and settled her against his own shoulder, then followed Beth inside to the narrow entry and on up the stairs.

"Why did you come back?" She knew the tone of accusation in her voice sounded sharp and petty, but she couldn't help it. "You were certainly in a rush to leave."

From behind her, she heard him sigh heavily. "I…was."

She kept moving on into Sophie's room, settled her in bed, then came out to the living room and leaned a shoulder against the wall, her arms folded. "Well?"

"I—" He fell silent for a moment, his eyes bleak. "I'm sorry. I should've stayed."

"I managed." Her voice was clipped. "So you really didn't need to come back."

He moved farther into the room, surveying the dark shadows, then turned back to face her. "Why were you afraid to answer the phone, Beth?"

His grim expression demanded answers she didn't want to give. Not if it meant stirring up his interest in her past. "I've…had a few prank calls," she hedged. "I don't know who—the caller ID always just says 'unknown.'"

That part was certainly true, at any rate.

She pivoted into the kitchen to start a pot of decaf. Part of her wanted to tell him everything, but what could he do, after all? The Chicago police certainly hadn't been any help.

"Did the calls start after you moved here, or before?" He soundlessly came up behind her, rested his large hands on her shoulders and gently turned her around.

"Well…" She sighed. "Before."

His eyes were troubled as he studied her face. "Same guy?"

She shrugged away his concern. "These days, it's all too easy to find a phone number on the Internet."

"Has he threatened you in any way?"

"Sort of."

*"Sort of?"*

"He threatened to come after me." She pulled back and turned to fill the coffeemaker reservoir, then pulled packages of filters and ground French roast from the cupboard. "But he probably doesn't even know where I live...exactly."

"No? Reverse lookup on the Internet will identify the address and name connected to almost any listed number. How did you list your new phone?"

"Crystal's Café, with the street address."

"Not your first and last name?"

"Nope." She measured out the coffee, then shut the lid on the coffeemaker and flipped the switch on.

"But information on property ownership is online, too. Public county records, in most states. He could probably figure out the address, since you and your sister have owned this place for a number of years."

"Five," she whispered, bracing her hands on the counter and bowing her head.

Joel shook his head slowly. "So we've established that this guy called you even before you moved here. He has made threats. And, with a little work, he could trace you right to your door."

A shiver ran down Beth's spine.

"Which then brings up the big question—who is he, and why would anyone want to bother you?"

SHE MANAGED TO HEDGE with vague replies and nonchalance, and breathed a sigh of relief when

Joel finally left. The dark look in his eyes promised that the subject was far from over, but what could she say? She didn't know who her caller was. The big-city cops hadn't been able to find him—and she'd seen the doubt in their eyes at any rate. Most of them probably figured the story was a weak cover for all the money Patrick had supposedly embezzled and hidden away.

And worse, her amateur investigation into Patrick's activities had apparently triggered her stalker in the first place. So now, if the guy caught wind of someone asking too many questions of people back in Chicago, there might be a chance that he could panic. And until she found what he was after—if the items even existed—she just couldn't risk it. Not for her sake, and especially not for Sophie's. What would she do if he arrived at her door and forced his way inside?

Just a few months of work on the café and the sale of the property, then she and Sophie would be on their way to Montana. And with that move, she'd be smarter. She'd rent a post office box, get an unlisted phone number and figure out a way to avoid leaving any other sort of trail someone could follow.

Too tense to think of sleeping, she called Melanie to discuss her progress on the remodeling, then she quietly tackled the remaining wallpaper, soaking it with a sponge and trying to pry up the edges with a scraper. It came away in slimy, thumbnail-sized bits, a painstaking process that kept her hands busy but her mind free to dwell on all the troubles ahead.

By three o'clock in the morning her arms and fingers ached, and bed was a welcome thought. *So much for that,* she muttered to herself. Bracing her hands at the small of her back, she ambled to the windows facing the street and lifted one for a breath of fresh air.

A dark sedan idled on the street, the dim glow of its instrument panel just visible, though its head-lights were turned off.

Across the street and to the north, there were only empty lots, and Canyon Street ended just a hundred feet past her house at a pasture fence. To the south, the vet clinic was closed. So why would anyone be out there at this time of night?

A minute later, the car eased away from the curb and disappeared into the darkness without ever turning its headlights on.

There was no basis for calling the cops—just a couple anonymous phone calls. An idling car that may have just held two lovers talking into the wee hours.

Beth sat at the window and kept watch until she couldn't keep her eyes open any longer, and then she drifted off into a troubled sleep.

IN THE MORNING, Beth awoke bleary-eyed but with new resolve. While Sophie slept, she found her to do list, and rewrote every one of the twenty tasks in order of revised importance for opening the café as soon as possible.

With the kitchen cupboards done, Joel had promised to tackle the plumbing problems next, followed by the installation of a small, commercial dishwasher. After that, she'd paint the kitchen a bright off-white and he could put down the vinyl flooring.

And when she wasn't working at the vet clinic or taking care of Sophie, she'd be scrubbing, painting and wallpapering the dining area itself. But first thing today, a local rubbish hauler was scheduled to stop by with his hulking son to finally clear out the junk in the yard.

Whistling, she opened the windows so she could hear if Sophie awakened and called her, then she hurried downstairs to survey the project one more time.

She opened the front door of the café to find the man and his son leaning against their truck, scowling.

"So what did you do," the older man growled, jingling his truck keys in one hand, "empty out the place and dump it in your yard?"

Mystified, she stepped outside onto the porch. "I know it's a big job…"

"Lady, this wasn't our deal." He motioned for his son to get back in the truck.

"Wait—" She hurried down the porch stairs. He snorted and climbed behind the wheel. *"Please!"*

And then she got a good look at her yard. From day one, there'd been the old VW car parts. A rusted-out car frame. Assorted junk thrown everywhere. She'd picked up most of the smaller things already, and had piled them neatly to one side.

But now, the yard was awash in garbage. Countless bulging black plastic bags filled with garbage, many of them ripped open. A brisk breeze sent old newspapers flying down the street.

The stack of refuse that she'd so carefully collected had been strewn across the yard, and in the center of her sidewalk was a pile of what could only be fresh cow manure.

Her hand at her mouth, she turned slowly…only to find the front of the café had been spray-painted with graffiti, in bright red.

The words were in Spanish, but even with her lack of fluency in the language, she knew the perpetrator had described her in the most graphic terms.

Backing up, she sank onto the porch steps, wavering between tears and anger. Her caller had given her ten days, and this just wasn't his style at any rate. So who else would want to cause her harm?

In a town this size, someone surely must have an idea about who could've done it. And this time, she was calling the sheriff.

## CHAPTER SEVEN

DAN TALBOT, the new sheriff, arrived a few hours later after being held up with a multicar accident on the highway in a distant part of the county. He appeared weary, dusty and not terribly impressed by the gravity of her problem when Beth gave him a tour of her yard.

She didn't blame him. After dealing with a fatality, this had to seem like a frivolous call.

His deputy, an older man named Randy with hard eyes and a belly that strained the buttons of his shirt, kicked through the piles of garbage and bent down now and then to survey certain pieces. "I'd say someone got this out at the landfill, boss. Lotsa different addresses on the envelopes. As for the manure, that could be from any one of a dozen ranches in the area."

"I want you to ask around town, Randy, and check with the neighbors," Talbot said. "Maybe someone saw something peculiar."

"There was a dark sedan parked out front early

this morning with its lights off," Beth said. "But I couldn't see the make and model. And anyway, a car couldn't have held all this trash."

He looked up from his clipboard, his pen poised. "Got any enemies in these parts? Anyone who might hold a grudge?"

"Not here. I haven't been here that long."

"Anyone who isn't happy about you opening this place? Neighbors, who've been angry over the condition of the property?"

"If they didn't like the mess, why would they make it worse?" She shook her head. "Walt is my closest neighbor and he's all for seeing this place cleaned up. There really aren't any other neighbors back here, and I haven't met many people yet. Just Walt, his nephew and the ladies at day care. I…just don't know anyone else."

She looked up to find Sheriff Talbot studying her intently. "Think of someone, ma'am?"

"I—I've had a crank caller…twice, since I moved here. But I have no idea who it is."

Talbot's gaze sharpened. "Is he threatening you?"

"Sort of, but I don't think it has anything to do with all of this." She debated about telling him the whole sordid story about Patrick, the embezzlement and the subsequent investigation, but there was really no point. "I think it's a guy who called a couple times when I was still in Chicago, but since the last call I don't think he could've made it down here that fast. And coming all that way to trash my yard just isn't plausible."

"People have done crazier things, ma'am. If this guy has a real vendetta going he could even find a way to hire someone. Do you have caller ID? Have you tried recording his calls?"

"Caller ID, yes—but he's always just used pay phones."

Talbot nodded thoughtfully. "I've got a gadget in my car—you can route your phone cord through it and attach a tape recorder, just in case he calls again. Not to say that he's the only suspect today. We'll do some checking with some high school boys, too. Maybe some of them had a little too much to drink and thought this would be a lark. I'm afraid it's happened a time or two before, though I thought most of the troublemakers here were grown and gone."

Frustration and rising anger made it hard to speak. "A lark? All of this would be a lark to them?"

"Stupid, I know." He wrote a few more notes. "If I find the responsible parties, you can bet they'll be facing charges and paying restitution."

If they were found, which seemed highly un-likely. "So in the meantime…"

"Loraine Gilbert doesn't live too far out of town, and I'll bet she has a tractor and a big hayrack you could use. I'll call and see if she'll have her hired man bring them into town so you can haul this stuff to the landfill." He studied the perimeter of her yard, where sections of an old wrought-iron fence had twisted and fallen from decades of neglect. "If I were you, I'd consider getting my fence up, then I'd invest in a good dog. At least you'd have some warning next time, before things go too far."

*Next time?* The thought of facing something like this again sent a shudder down her spine. Beth mentally added fence fixing and dog shopping to her to do list. "And that's it? That's all you can do?"

Talbot shrugged. "If we find out who did it, we'll arrest them for trespassing and vandalism. Maybe one of them will brag about it, or someone saw something suspicious, and word will spread. But honestly, don't count on it."

"That's just depressing."

"Most people don't even lock their doors around here, but maybe you'll want to look at a security system." He studied her for a moment, then shook his head. "Someone went to a lot of trouble here. That tells me it was probably more than just a teenage prank—and ups the likelihood that they just might come back."

TALBOT HELPED HER attach a tape recorder to the café phone, and the tractor and wagon appeared by late morning, parked in front of her house. After sending Sophie to Gina's house for her play date with Olivia, Beth donned a pair of leather gloves and got to work. When Walt arrived with a half-dozen teenagers to help, she could have kissed his feet.

"Saturday mornings are quiet around here," he said with a benevolent smile as he watched them tackle the mess. "And jobs are hard to come by. Don't worry, though—I promised fifty bucks to their youth group at church, and they were more than happy to help."

"I'll pay them, Walt. I'm just thrilled that you were able to get them here."

He waved away her offer. "Consider it a gift. I've got to get over to the clinic for my Saturday morning appointments, but I think you'd best stay here and supervise."

"Gladly." She nearly gave in to the temptation to give him a hug of thanks. "By the way, have you seen Joel? He was going to install my dishwasher."

"Nope." Walt glanced at his watch. "He had to run up to Austin early this morning after some light fixtures for my office. He won't be back until evening."

BY TWO O'CLOCK, the front and back yards were spotless, save for the larger car parts and the rusted VW, and the rubbish hauler agreed to pick up those things on Monday. Beth tipped the teenagers an extra twenty dollars for pizza, then collapsed on a wrought-iron bench in the front yard, exhausted.

When Gina's red Tahoe pulled up a few minutes later, Beth hobbled out to the curb to get Sophie out of her car seat. As soon as she was free, Sophie flew into Beth's arms, her face alight with joy. "I had fun, Momma! We played games and dolls, and we had lunch…and they have a waterslide!"

"I hope you don't mind," Gina said with a smile. "It's one of those long plastic things with water jets. There's nothing more fun than getting wet on a warm day."

"I'm just thrilled that Sophie got to visit." Beth bent down to peer into the empty front and back seats of the vehicle. "Did everything go all right?"

"The girls played nonstop." Gina's smile faded. "I had to drop Olivia off at her dad's place on the way over here, though. He's got her the rest of the weekend."

"That's got to be so tough." What would it be like, going back to a house that echoed with loneliness for an entire weekend? "Would you like to come in for some tea?"

"I can't. I have a meeting at church…." Her eyes widened as she took in the front yard. "Holy cow— what a difference!"

"The troops landed this morning, and they left just a few minutes ago." Beth closed her eyes briefly. "I cannot thank those kids enough for all they did. If I hadn't promised to go to the Lone Wolf Spring Festival tonight, I'd just sit right here and enjoy looking at my clean yard."

"So you've got a hot date?" Gina teased.

Beth rolled her eyes. "More of a mercy date, really. On both counts."

"Okay, now you *have* to tell me."

"Nothing much to tell. I think Joel wanted a human shield, so some of the overeager, match-making mothers in town will back off. And...well, a widowed mom with scars and a limp isn't much of a prize. I just figured it would be a chance to get out for a few hours."

Gina looked appalled. "You make yourself sound old as Methuselah. What are you, child, pushing thirty?"

"Thirty-two."

Gina propped her fists on her hips and surveyed Beth from head to toe. "And *what* scars?" She leaned closer and gently touched Beth's cheek. "You can't mean these faint ones here."

"A person can hardly miss them." Beth pushed back the sleeve of her shirt to show off the scars on her arm. "Or these. Makes the classic little black cocktail dress a challenge, don't you think?"

"If it's sleeveless, maybe, but not all of them are—and that isn't what people wear to these affairs, anyway." Gina tapped her lips with a neatly manicured forefinger. "Nice slacks and tops. Or spring dresses. Long sleeves would be fine, or you could add a pretty cashmere pashmina."

Beth glanced down at her T-shirt and old jeans. "I'm afraid I left the country club life back in Chicago."

"That's *it?* Just jeans and shirts?"

"Mostly. With a few skirts and sweaters thrown in."

"Well, babe, you are in luck today. Auntie Gina gained an unfortunate amount of weight after her divorce, and she has a whole wardrobe in the wrong size."

JOEL TOOK ONE LOOK at Beth, and nearly choked on his spearmint gum.

Even in jeans and T-shirts, she'd looked trim and attractive, but in a body-hugging, rose-colored dress that didn't begin to reach her knees and those silvery, high-heeled shoes, she looked incredible. Sexy.

And she was exactly what he'd been hoping to avoid.

The good thing was that the women who'd been flirting with him would see that he was unavailable, and he wouldn't need to flounder for tactful, distancing conversation.

The bad thing was that somehow he needed to keep his hands off Beth and remind himself that she was simply his friend and nothing more. She'd made that clear all along, and that had suited him perfectly…until now.

What was it about those delicate sandals that made her slender legs look even more provocative? Or that fabric, which seemed to glow with a life all its own as it caressed each one of her delicate curves?

Shaking off his reverie, he looked up and found that she was watching him with an uncertain expression in her eyes.

"These aren't my clothes," she murmured. "If you think I've overdressed or not well enough, just say the word. Gina said I'd be okay, but…"

He exhaled slowly. "*Okay?* You look fantastic."

"I wouldn't go that far, but thanks." She shot a teasing look at him. "Sophie said I looked almost as nice as her Princess Pony, so I'll go with that."

If Princess Pony looked half as good as Beth, the franchise had to be worth a mint. "Did she mind you leaving for the night?"

"Gina invited her over for the evening, so I imagine they're watching movies and baking cookies by now."

The sounds of an excellent oldies band wafted through the trees from where Main Street was cordoned off for a dance.

He'd planned to maintain a casual sort of distance, but he'd been outraged to learn of the damage done to Beth's property, and with that anger had come an overwhelming surge of protectiveness. Now, it simply felt natural and right to take Beth's hand as they walked the two blocks to downtown.

And once they hit the edge of the crowd, draping his arm around her waist seemed only…*practical,* so they wouldn't end up separated.

Beth's eyes widened when they reached the edge of the crowd. "Where on earth did all these people come from?"

"From all over the county, probably. Small-town affairs always draw a good crowd." He leaned down and drew her closer to be heard over a Beach Boys classic. "Want to dance?"

"Nope."

"Please?"

"Remember our deal? If I don't dance, no one has to be embarrassed about how truly awful I am."

But when a slow dance came up, he held out a hand anyway. "Please? It's been years since I did this, so *I'll* probably embarrass you all to pieces. But I'd sure like to try just one dance, if you wouldn't mind."

She hesitated, a blush tinting her cheeks. "I— can't."

"Just here—in the shadows?" He gently pulled her into his arms, and she tentatively followed him. Stiffly at first, and then she relaxed into a slow and sensual sway to the intimate rhythm, dropping her head against his shoulder and locking her hands behind his neck.

She smelled faintly of some sort of floral shampoo and another light, flowery scent that he couldn't quite identify. The crowd seemed to fade away as he absorbed her warmth against his chest.

He wanted the music to last forever.

Then somehow, he found himself lifting her chin with a forefinger and dropping a kiss on her mouth. A tentative kiss, and then one that was deeper. Longer. More potent. He slid a hand down to the small of her back, pulling her closer—

"Howdy, son." Walt's booming voice broke through the spell with the finesse of a loose bull in a flower bed. "Great to see you here!"

Beth pulled back, her expression dazed, her lips swollen.

"Um…glad to see you, too," Joel muttered.

"Sorry I interrupted." His eyes twinkled. "Guess I'd better head over to the barbecue tent, and let you enjoy the dance—unless you want to join me and Loraine for a mighty good supper." He glanced at his watch. "She oughta be here soon."

Joel *wanted* to go home and take Beth with him, so he could do a little more exploring of her exquisite mouth, but that was a bad idea. Then another slow dance started, and there was no contest between supper and a chance to draw her into his arms once again. "Maybe later, Walt."

This time, she didn't hesitate quite as long when he asked her to dance. "Wonderful," he murmured. "It's been so long since I've done this."

"Heavenly."

She followed his lead, her body perfectly molded to his, through two more songs. But when the band switched into a rollicking rock-and-roll song, she backed out of his arms with a firm shake of her head. "I don't think I can manage that just yet. It's time to join your uncle for that barbecue, don't you think?"

The answer was no, but she was right. That barbecue was a lot safer than slow dancing his way into trouble. What had he been thinking, when he asked Beth out? It hadn't really been about the other women who'd been pursuing him with their daughters and nieces, because he could handle that. And he hadn't just been thinking about delving deeper into Beth's past, either, on the pretext of keeping Walt's finances safe.

Nope—he'd been thinking about her smile. How much fun it was to talk to her, and tease her a little. And it was about how he was coming to admire her strength and resolve while she dealt with the loss of her husband, the raising of her little girl alone and the monumental project she was undertaking at Crystal's Café.

And maybe he'd been thinking about a whole lot more. He couldn't even remember the last time he'd spent a night with a woman, and Beth was stirring up all sorts of thoughts in that direction.

But it was a direction he wouldn't be going. Certainly not toward anything serious, and anything less would be unfair to her. She was the kind of woman who inspired thoughts of settling down, and he would never risk that kind of commitment again.

With a deep sigh, Joel glanced at the dancers one last time, then followed her through the crowd.

SOPHIE WRAPPED HER ARMS around Beth's neck for her good-night kiss. "Can I go to Olivia's house again someday?"

"I'm sure you can, sweetheart. And as soon as we've got things in better shape here, we'll invite her over. Okay?"

Sophie nodded, rubbing her eyes. After her prayers, Beth gave her another kiss and tucked her in, then turned on her night-light and quietly slipped out of her room.

Silvery moonlight filtered through the curtains, casting the living room in deep shadows. She curled up in the window seat with an afghan and rested her head against the window frame.

Coyotes howled in the distance, and from one of the tall live oaks in the yard, an owl hooted. Lonely sounds that echoed the wistful feelings in her heart.

*What* had she been thinking? Sure, she'd declined Joel's invitation initially, but then she'd given in, figuring they were both adults. Figuring that she could keep this evening on a superficial, friendly basis. The two of them, just pals. Buddies. And after the vandalism at this place, she'd hardly been in a festive mood.

But then he'd eased her out in the crowd during that wonderfully romantic Bill Medley song from *Dirty Dancing,* and she'd melted into his arms.

He'd made her feel as if she were the most desirable woman on the planet, his attention totally riveted on her, and his large, warm hand at the small of her back, as if he wanted to absorb her into himself.

Never had she felt such intense male focus. Such need to take it to the next level. If dear old Walt hadn't jarred her back to reality, she just might've done something truly embarrassing, because she'd completely zoned out the others dancing in the street.

It was as if she and Joel were the only ones there.

How on earth had he done that? And with her—prim, proper Beth Lindstrom, who was hardly the stuff of any man's fantasies.

Yet during that incredible moment at the street dance, Joel's kiss had promised passion and wild abandon and more. She'd never felt so cherished, so safe and protected.

But he'd put on the brakes when his uncle showed up, and she had, too. Then they'd delved into a wonderful barbecue with Walt and Loraine, listening to the music until the band finally packed up for the night.

Walt's clients spanned two counties, and they all seemed to be there tonight. Many of them wandered by for a brief conversation.

They'd politely talked to her and Joel, too…mentioning future construction projects and asking for his business card. Expressing interest in the café, and asking how she was progressing with the building, or offering condolences about the graffiti incident.

They were warm, friendly folks. Small-town folks with connections to each other that ran deep, and generations of shared experiences that made them truly belong to this town, and to each other, with a sense of belonging that she'd never felt in the city.

With each passing day she fell deeper into the quiet, laid-back rhythm of this town. What would it be like to stay here forever, to become a part of that fabric? It called to her in an elemental way. Maybe…if all went well with the café, she and Sophie could stay here for good.

# CHAPTER EIGHT

BETH DUSTED OFF HER HANDS, walked backward to the curb and studied the house with a critical eye.

During the three weeks since the street dance, she'd thrown herself into renovating the place, imagining the day when she could reopen the café and start building a future for Sophie and herself in this town. Keeping busy had also helped distract her from her anonymous caller's threat about "ten days or less," though that deadline had come and gone without another word.

The exterior now sported pale yellow paint with crisp white trim around the windows and doors. The front door itself was a cheerful, bright blue, with *Crystal's* painted in bold diagonal script.

She'd planned on doing the painting later, but covering the dark graffiti had entailed so many coats of paint that she'd finally given up trying to match new and faded yellows, and did the whole thing.

She'd also added deep-blue window boxes filled

with crimson geraniums, and white, half-barrel planters of geraniums at either side of the steps leading up to the front covered porch.

Though she would have preferred lace, she'd saved that for the family quarters upstairs and had hung oyster-white vertical blinds at all of the main floor windows, opting for an effect that wouldn't make the local cowboys cringe.

Frowning, she turned to Gina. "Does it work? The colors, I mean."

Standing next to her, Gina grinned and gave her a quick hug. "Perfect. And it isn't too froufrou for the ranchers, either. So…can I have the inside tour?"

Beth hadn't let anyone but Joel and Sophie into the café for the past several weeks. Now, she led her friend up the stairs, opened the front door and ushered her inside.

"Oooh," Gina breathed. She took a few more steps, then slowly turned, her eyes wide. "I love the blue gingham wallpaper. And the white wainscoting—perfect!"

"It's three-inch vertical pine, and just what I wanted. Joel found it in a house that was being torn down out in the country." She nodded toward a smaller, more private dining area in the back. "He found those French doors out there, too."

Gina ran a hand over one of the tabletops set with gingham place mats. "Who refinished all of these tables?"

"Mostly me, then Joel had to pitch in. Sanding the tables and chairs was far more work than I thought. He did the oak flooring, too." Beth flexed her aching hands. "I just wish Crystal could see what we've done here. She was always so proud of her café."

Beth led Gina back to the kitchen, which now sported large fluorescent lights, gleaming fixtures and clean white walls. "The state inspectors came yesterday, so starting Monday, we'll be in business. I'll still be able to work at the clinic for a few hours in the late afternoons, though. The steady money will come in handy."

"Sounds like you and Joel make a great team." Gina gave Beth a sidelong glance. "Any news in that department?"

Beth rolled her eyes. "Of course not. He's been doing a wonderful job for me and has charged half what he should have. I'm grateful, but that's as far as anything goes."

She'd had to remind herself of that every day.

Going to the town's celebration had seemed like a reasonable favor to grant. She and Joel had reached an easy sort of working relationship by then, and it had sounded like a pleasant night out— the first she'd had since Patrick's death.

She hadn't foreseen the incredible impact of those slow dances in his arms. The heat of his kiss.

Or the fact that they'd end up in such an awkward situation afterward—that cautious, carefully superficial mode between two people who'd gone a little too far and instantly regretted it.

Now she was careful to avoid inadvertent contact, and tried for only the most innocuous conversations, for fear that he'd misconstrue her actions as those of a love-hungry widow.

He seemed even more cautious than she did—and was probably terrified that she was going to pursue him like the other women in town did.

"...so, I think you two should fall head over heels in love, get married and stay right here in Lone Wolf," Gina continued, gently elbowing Beth in the ribs. "Who will I go garage-saling with when you leave?"

Beth pulled herself back into the present. "Honestly, I'll miss you, too, if I move away."

She gazed at the Russell and Wyeth prints on the walls, and the collection of old chintz and calico teapots she'd brought with her from Chicago on a white hutch along the east wall. Even the extra tables and chairs had been bargain finds during the Saturdays she and Gina had gone treasure hunting.

It had been years since she'd had the freedom to spend time with friends.

Gina strolled across the room to the old-fashioned soda fountain, with its long marble counter and tall, red upholstered stools. "So what's left, then?"

"Just a few things upstairs. Varnishing. Wallpapering. A new area rug. More insulation up in the attic to help with the summer heat and chilly winters." Beth sighed. "And then…I guess I'll start checking out the Realtors in the area. If the café brings in some good business, it should help me get a good price. Or, it might even make staying here a possibility."

"I hope so. The thought of you leaving still makes me sad." Gina grimaced as she glanced at her watch. "I'd better run, because I need to pick up Olivia at her dad's place by noon. The less she's around his new girlfriend, the better."

Another reason, among many, why being single was proving to be a very satisfactory way to live.

Beth followed Gina out to the street, waved goodbye, then settled on the front porch swing to thumb through the stack of mail she'd picked up at the post office.

A fistful of credit-card applications destined for the shredder.

The local paper, which came out Saturdays and Wednesdays.

A letter from her sister, Melanie.

At the bottom of the stack, the official-looking letter that she'd had to sign for, from the county attorney's office in Chicago.

Her hand trembled as she slid a finger under the flap.

There'd been a lot of questions after Patrick's

death. Over the timing of the accident. Problems at the construction company, where he'd worked in accounting. Still numb with shock and in pain from her injuries, she'd had no answers to give, though she'd seen the doubt and suspicion in the eyes of the investigators.

The break-in at her home a few weeks later brought them all back again, but in the end, they'd finally gone away and had left her in relative peace...though some of their wild suppositions about Patrick's activities gnawed at her.

Even if none of it made any sense.

She finished opening the envelope and spread the letter out against her knees.

This letter is to inform you that the investigation into the charges filed against Patrick Martin Lindstrom has been reopened. We may need to obtain further statements from you.

She stared at the letter. Read it twice. Then folded it back into the envelope, her stomach tying itself in knots. *So it still isn't over.*

And things weren't much better here. According to the sheriff, his interviews with the troublesome teenagers he'd called "his usual suspects" had yielded alibis for all three on the night her yard was trashed. They'd mentioned seeing a local, unemployed man named Hubie Post lurking in the vicinity earlier that evening, though Talbot hadn't been able to track him down for questioning. *Hubie*. Wasn't he the guy who'd been sent to help her move in, but never showed up?

The thought gave her a chill. What about the mysterious car that occasionally crept down Canyon Street late at night—was there an innocent explanation for why it idled in that dark and deserted area? And why in the world would a vagrant like Hubie bother to vandalize her yard? It just didn't make sense.

Yet lately, she'd begun to have the eerie sensation that she was being watched…and the two late-night phone calls last month certainly hadn't been her imagination. Innocuous problems, compared to the threat that her caller made, though he'd given her that warning a month ago and hadn't ever turned up. Since then it had been hard to sleep at night.

She rose, dusted off her jeans and glanced over at the vet clinic parking lot.

It was time to pay Walt another visit.


"I WANT TO THANK YOU again for Darwin," Beth began, setting a coconut cream cake on the counter in the vet clinic. "He is one fabulous cat."

Walt lifted an eyebrow. "You're bringing him back?"

"Only if you need him. Sophie loves him and he terrifies the mice, so it's a perfect relationship in every way."

"Then he's yours." Walt chuckled. "I was hoping you'd want him."

"Now I need a dog. Something noisy. Fierce. Something that will frighten away strangers but be dependable with Sophie…and not eat my café customers if they happen to intersect."

Walt's brow furrowed. "You think those vandals will come back?"

"I hope not. But the sheriff recommended a dog a while back, and I believe he's right. There's not another house for almost two blocks, and when the clinic is closed this is a pretty lonely area."

"You *like* dogs? They need a lot of love and attention."

"My husband never let me have one, but I grew up with goldens. Now that Joel has finished the fence around my property, it's time to start looking." She smiled, hoping her anxiety didn't show. If Walt picked up on it, he would talk to Joel, and then she'd face the third degree from both of them. "He fixed it so the front and back yards are completely fenced, but can be closed off from each other. Sophie could use a buddy," she added.

"Well…the goldens I know would probably lick an intruder to death, but they'd be great with Sophie." He pondered for a minute, then smiled. "I do

know of something that just might work. Loraine's
uncle Kenny recently moved into a care center, and
has to give up his dog. It isn't really a ranch sort of
dog, so it isn't working out too well for Loraine to
keep her."

Beth envisioned a doddering, gray-muzzled dog
that would provide protection only if an intruder
happened to trip over it on the way into the house.
"Is it…lively?"

"Enough."

"Is it *old?*"

"Middle-aged."

"Big?"

"Not very."

"Housebroken?"

"I'm sure she is." He smiled. "I'll bring Viper
over tonight and let you take a look."

She felt herself pale. "V-Viper?"

Walt chuckled. "You just need to meet her, and
see what you think."

*She came over today asking for a watchdog,* Walt
had said. *Maybe you should see if she's in some
kind of trouble over there.*

Walt was still blatantly attempting to bring Joel
and Beth together as a couple, so asking Joel to
check in on her could be just another ploy. Yet, Walt
did worry about everyone who came under his
wing, and it certainly seemed plausible that Beth

could be in trouble. From her first day in town, Joel had sensed an undercurrent of wariness in her manner that had piqued his curiosity.

Her husband's death…her anonymous caller… the vandalism at her place—did it all add up to more than she'd been willing to reveal? Had she been in some sort of serious trouble before moving here? All things considered, Joel would bet his badge—if he still had one—that there was something in her past that she wanted hidden.

It was definitely time to call in an old favor.

He flipped open his cell phone, and punched in the number of an investigator he knew in Detroit. The phone rang six times before rolling into voice mail. "Hey, Steve. I've got a favor to ask. I need a background check on a woman from Chicago…and her late husband."

JOEL CHECKED HIS voice and e-mail messages every twenty minutes, impatient for an answer. Maybe his hunch was wrong. But if it wasn't, Beth and her daughter might well be in danger living alone in that drafty old house. His blood chilled at the thought of them staying there, defenseless and at the mercy of the slow response times of the overtaxed sheriff's department, with so few officers trying to cover the entire county.

He paced the length of his house another time, then went back to his office and glared at the computer monitor. Maybe Steve was out on a case. Maybe he was on a vacation, or had left early for the day and wouldn't even be listening to his messages. Maybe—

The computer chimed, and the mailbox flag started waving at the bottom of his monitor screen. He quickly clicked into Yahoo and found the newest incoming mail. *Bingo.*

The message from Steve was terse. He'd also attached copies of several archived articles from the *Chicago Tribune.*

The pencil in Joel's hand snapped as he read them. He hit Print, then impatiently waited for the paper to shoot out of the laser printer.

In less than two minutes he was heading for town, Steve's words still hitting him with the staccato impact of semiautomatic gunfire.

Maybe he and Beth had only known each other for a couple months, but she was a woman alone, and he'd thought they were friends by now. Why hadn't she trusted him enough to tell him the truth?

He thought about sweet little Sophie, defenseless and trusting. And Beth, who'd have no chance against a thug who might easily be twice her size.

He was going to pay Beth a visit, and he was going to lay things on the line, to just see what she had to say. But all the way to town, he prayed Steve's message was wrong.

WALT SET the pet carrier down on Beth's porch and beamed at her. "I think," he said with a broad smile, "that Viper here is the answer to your dilemma."

Beth eyed the carrier, unable to conceal her doubt. "It...must be so *small*."

"Can I see, Momma? Please?" Sophie struggled in Beth's arms, wanting to get down.

But small or not, anything by the name of Viper had to present some risk to tiny fingers and toes.

"Hang on, honey, until we see what this is." She looked at Walt. "Are you sure this dog will be imposing enough?"

He leaned down and unlatched the door. "Take a look."

A pointy black nose appeared.

Thick, short black fur.

Beady little eyes.

Then ears similar to a fox...or a bat. A bristly black lion's ruff of a mane, then a short, compact body without a tail. It couldn't possibly weigh more than eight or nine pounds.

Disappointment washed through her. "Wh-what is it?"

"A Schipperke."

"But it's...it's *small*."

"She *thinks* she weighs a good sixty pounds. This dog will settle the score on any dog that gets in her way—it absolutely terrorized Loraine's two Australian shepherds."

She couldn't conceal her doubt. "I'm not sure—"

Walt chuckled. "With this thick, black coat, she's practically invisible in the dark, unless she bares her teeth. She took down a burglar, once. Nailed him in the ankles, barked enough to raise the dead, and had him cornered and trembling 'til the cops arrived."

"So she's mean."

"These dogs are very protective of their homes and family. They bark up a storm if there's a threat, and believe me, any intruder would think twice about risking that kind of notice." He picked up the dog and cuddled her against his chest. "She was raised around Kenny's grandkids, so she should be fine with Sophie. You should probably keep her in the backyard when the café is open, though, in case she assumes your customers are trying to break in."

That didn't sound good, but Walt had been right about the cat....

"Then I guess we could give this a try," Beth said faintly. She put Sophie down, and reached out to stroke the top of the dog's head. Viper's long, pink tongue swooped out to lick her hand. "You're sure she'll be good with us? Predictable?"

He chuckled fondly as he placed the dog in Beth's arms. "Give her a day or so to make herself at home, and I'll guarantee it. I promise you, she'll protect this place with her life."

JOEL PULLED TO A HALT in the alley behind Beth's house and jogged to the backyard gate.

He'd barely touched the latch when something small and black burst off the porch and flew down the walk like a supersonic bowling ball—barking loud enough to alert the entire county. It threw itself against the gate, needle sharp teeth snapping as it jumped higher and higher, apparently trying to gain enough altitude to make it over the gate and take him out.

His ears ringing, he took a step back and looked up to find Beth out on the porch, hands on her hips. She shook her head in apparent amazement, then placed two fingers at her lips and whistled sharply. "C'mon, Viper. It's okay."

The dog backed off growling, its eyes riveted on Joel's. Daring him, in no uncertain terms, to make the next move.

But when Beth whistled again, it turned and trotted up the walk to sit in front of her.

"I still don't think I'm coming in," he said, trying to keep a straight face. "What is that thing, anyway?"

Beth picked up the doglet and rubbed it behind the ears. "A gift from your uncle. I think it works."

He drew close to Beth and offered his open palm to the dog. It looked up at him, seemed to judge him a friend, then licked his hand. "What about Sophie?"

"I've been watching them really close, but they seem fine together." She put the dog down and watched as it bounded back into the yard to bark at a squirrel. "Darwin's another story. He took one look at Viper, jumped from the top of the refrigerator and gave her a glare that could've melted steel. Now and then he comes down to parade in front of her nose, just to let her know who's boss."

Beth wore a soft pink top that barely skimmed the waist of her matching shorts, and her long, strawberry blond hair was loose and curly today. From all appearances, someone might guess she was Sophie's high school babysitter...too fresh and innocent to ever be involved in anything illegal.

He caught her delicate scent—like sweet, lush peaches, this time—on a soft breeze.

And just like that, his steely resolution to confront her started melting fast as ice under the hot Texas sun.

Since the night of the dance he hadn't been able to stop thinking about the intense emotions he'd felt, just holding her in his arms. He hadn't meant to kiss her, but it had been as natural as breathing to lower his mouth to hers.

Just the moonlight, he'd told himself.

The intimacy of holding a woman close.

*Any* woman, after such a long time alone.

But that brief, innocent kiss had totally blown him away. In an instant, the music and the moonlight and the crowd pressing against them had faded. His focus had narrowed down to Beth's warmth. Her softness. Her sweet, inviting mouth, and the way she'd responded.

She tempted him more than anyone had since the bitter end of his marriage, but he hadn't been a cop for nearly fifteen years for nothing.

He was going to find out what her secrets were...so he could help her, in case danger arrived at her door.

## CHAPTER NINE

A SHIVER OF UNEASE SWEPT through Beth at the intense expression in Joel's dark eyes.

From the moment they'd met, he'd seemed a little too interested in her past. He'd made her feel edgy, uncertain. They'd settled into a comfortable working relationship—friendship, even—marred only by that sensual, slow dance from heaven, and an incredible kiss that she'd tried to forget.

But now, she could see his doubts about her were back a hundredfold.

She fixed a bright, breezy smile on her face. "If you're concerned about the upstairs appliances, they won't be coming until the fifth of June. I can have Sears do those installations. I'm just thankful for all you've done with the café. My food supplier will be making the first delivery tomorrow, and I can open on Wednesday, just as planned. I even have the—"

"Beth."

She turned away, unable to meet his eyes any

longer, and bent to hunt for dead blooms on the geraniums by the steps. "Um...do I owe you more money? If I do, I'll settle up on Friday. Unless you need it now? I can—"

"I don't want your money. I just want some answers."

She snapped off a dead bloom. Then two more, and tossed them out in the yard. "Answers?"

"Beth, look at me."

He drew closer, and she caught the woodsy, faint fragrance of his aftershave. The clean scent of Dial soap. She reached for another faded flower, but instead of it breaking off, the entire stem tore away.

"You can trust me," he added quietly.

She shot a quick glance at him, then picked at the petals of the blossom in her hand. "We're doing great, thanks to you. The café is ready to open, and the apartment is almost done, too. You've done beautiful work."

"That's not what I mean."

He rested his hands on her shoulders, which sent a shiver through her of an entirely different kind. One totally out of place, especially now.

If he knew, others in Lone Wolf could find out, too, and what might those past accusations do to the future of the café and her job at the clinic? Her ability to provide for Sophie, and to make a new life for them both in Montana? Her financial status was already on rocky ground.

Joel felt the tension in her shoulders, and saw the rigid set of her jaw. Maybe she was in even more trouble than he'd guessed.

"You told me about the threatening phone calls." He turned her around to face him and gently lifted her chin. "The whole town knows about the graffiti incident, and how some jerk trashed your yard. But that's not the whole story, is it?"

She bit her lower lip. Her eyes darkened as she met his gaze and then looked away.

"When the phone rang at the café, I saw how scared you were. You were afraid the caller was someone else, yet you said you had no idea who it could be."

"I don't. Not for sure, anyway."

"Any reason why someone would target you?"

When she didn't answer, he withdrew the copies of the *Tribune* articles from his back pocket and handed them to her. "I'd guess this is a pretty good clue."

She skimmed the first one, then read it all again more slowly. But instead of fear or guilt, he could only detect anger flashing in her eyes. "Where did you get this?"

"Walt told me you were asking for a—a—" He looked down at the strange creature at her feet. "Whatever that is, for protection. He was concerned about you, and wanted me to look into the situation. Since I still have friends back in the Detroit PD, I asked one of them to do some checking. If someone was threatening you, I figured it was better to know. Logical?"

Her eyes narrowed. "So you investigated me."

"Steve checked your legal history, and you came up fine, actually. Not even a traffic ticket in the past ten years. But he did find these newspaper articles about your husband's death, and the investigation that followed."

She shoved the papers back into his hands. "The auditors at his company said several hundred thousand dollars were missing, and they decided he did it. It sure was convenient, blaming a dead man who couldn't defend himself."

He paused, giving her a chance to collect herself. "Did they question you about all of this?"

"Of course they did," she said bitterly. "They figured I must've helped him hide the money in a safe place, so therefore I could help them get it back." She glared at Joel and backed away. "But if that were true, I sure wouldn't be struggling to make ends meet, would I? I knew our house was mortgaged to the roof. But just before he died, Patrick emptied our bank accounts and maxed our credit cards on cash advances. I didn't know any of that until after his death."

"The cops probably assumed you two were filtering it all into some offshore account so you could flee the country."

"Exactly. Pat called home from work on the day

of the accident. Said he had a surprise weekend for the three of us, so I should pack quickly and be ready. But far as I knew, I was not getting ready to *run.*"

She turned on her heel to go back in the house, but Joel gently caught her arm. "Wait."

"To be tried and convicted by you? The authorities found no proof. I was never charged." Her voice rose, laced with the pain of betrayal and humiliation. "If anything, they probably thought I was pathetically stupid for not knowing what was going on."

The dog took an aggressive stance at Joel's feet, a low, threatening growl rumbling in its throat.

"Tell your dog," he said quietly, "to settle down. We need to talk, not get all upset."

"Upset?" Her eyes flashed fire. "How do you think I should feel when someone assumes the worst?"

"Believe me, I just want to help." He led her over to the porch swing and sat down next to her.

The dog followed and glared up at him, clearly eager to take things to the next level.

"I can just imagine." The rigidity of her spine seemed to fade, and now he saw only defeat in her eyes. "You know what will happen, now? Rumors will snowball. How can I possibly try to start a business here once that happens?"

"I don't intend to start any rumors, but word will probably get out sometime, and then you can calmly deal with it just as you did now. With the truth." He took one of her hands in his to offer comfort. Her hand was trembling and cold, and the desire to protect her welled in his chest. "But in the meantime, you've got bigger problems—and you need some answers."

"Tell me about it."

"The money situation and the car accident have to be related." He fought the urge to reach out and tuck a stray curl behind her ear. "It's all too coincidental, otherwise."

She nodded.

"What if there *was* an embezzlement scheme? Maybe Patrick found out about it, and threatened to go to the police. Or maybe he was involved against his will. Someone could've trapped him into cooperating, or got their hooks into him when he was weak. Maybe he wanted out, and the others were afraid he'd squeal."

She bowed her head. "The police asked me if he was suicidal, knowing he'd be caught and sent to prison. Maybe our marriage had problems, but I'll never believe that he'd kill himself and try to take Sophie and me with him."

"Did they find any evidence of tampering on your car?"

"None—though how they could tell, I don't know. I saw it at the junkyard after I got out of the hospital. The front left quadrant was crumpled like

aluminum foil, and the rest of the car nearly unrec-
ognizable."

"Any evidence of another car at the scene?"

"No." She looked away, her eyes glittering with
unshed tears. "The report said there were no foreign
paint marks, chips or unexplained damage. It claimed
that Patrick suddenly, inexplicably veered off the
highway. Our car went airborne over an embank-
ment, then rocketed into a concrete bridge abutment."

"Maybe someone veered in front of you. The lack
of physical evidence doesn't prove anything, does
it?"

"To the police, it did." Her voice trailed away.
"They said there would've been skid marks. Evidence that he'd slammed on the brakes, and steered
wildly to avoid impact. But still, there are Sophie's
nightmares...."

"Maybe she saw something and just doesn't
remember. Lots of people blank out during an
accident."

"I sure did, and I regret it every day," Beth retorted
bitterly. She reached into her back pocket and
handed Joel a folded envelope. "And the authorities
aren't done with me yet. They still believe I have the
loot stashed away in some secret hideaway."

He opened the letter and scanned the contents.
"They want another statement?"

"Probably because they hope to trip me up and
prove me a liar." She fidgeted with the wedding ring

on her right hand. "And what else can I tell them but the truth—again?"

"Did Patrick ever seem unusually tense or distracted, or mention any unexpected investments?"

"During the months before he died, he was more distant. He got defensive when I asked him what was wrong. But I suspected an affair, not this." A sad smile tipped up a corner of her mouth. "An affair would have been so much better. Now, it's not only the authorities who doubt me. Someone else is sure I have the money or know how to find it. And he could be anyone—someone at the company. A partner in crime. Or just some random person who has heard about it. And someday, his threats may actually be real."

AFTER AWAKENING AT THREE on Wednesday morning to bake her brioche, croissants and other assorted pastries, Beth changed aprons and flipped on the café lights. At seven o'clock she turned the front window sign to Open for the very first time.

At seven-fifteen she started pacing. Adjusting a picture frame here. The angle of a decorative teapot there.

At seven-thirty, she heard Sophie call her name, and she hurried upstairs for the morning ritual of hugs and kisses, then quickly dressed her and brought her down to the café for breakfast.

Two red-faced young cowboys—early twenties

at the most—stood just inside the front door, their hats held at their sides, their booted feet shuffling awkwardly.

They both looked as if they were about to bolt.

"Hi, guys, ready for breakfast?" Beth crossed the room to grab menus from an antique fern pedestal just inside the door.

They glanced at each other, both taking a wary step back at her approach. The taller one swallowed hard and nodded.

She smiled, suddenly realizing why they were here. "Ahhhh. You wouldn't be related to Gina Carlton, would you?"

The short one ducked his head. "Yes, ma'am. She's our aunt. I'm Charley, and this here is Jake."

Sophie came up beside her. "Are they *cowboys, Momma?*"

"Sure looks like it." Beth ruffled the crown of Sophie's head, then led the two men to a table by the front window, their boots clomping hollowly across the oak floor. She handed them each a menu. "Coffee, for starters?"

They both seemed entranced by the breakfast menu, and it took a moment for one of them to nod.

She brought them each a cup and left the small pot, then settled Sophie at a table in the back corner with her usual Cheerios, milk and juice, adding a sliced strawberry garnish to the cereal.

The two cowboys were still studying the menu

when she returned. Jake was talking furtively on his cell phone. "All set?"

They each shot a guilty look at her, then looked back at the menu.

"Can I help you decide? The pastries are all fresh baked. The brioche are still warm, in fact. Do you like omelets? The three-cheese with asparagus and dill is a good choice. Or," she added when Charley flinched, "there's the bacon and cheddar."

"I'll take that," Jake said quickly.

Charlie nodded. "Me, too."

"With the brioche, or a croissant?"

"That first one." They spoke nearly in unison.

She suppressed the sudden urge to give them both a hug, then glanced around the café as she headed to the kitchen.

Surely it didn't seem too feminine and intimidating...did it? The blue gingham was cheery and bright. Countrified, if anything. The white vertical blinds weren't the least bit fussy. The collection of chintz teapots was a pretty touch over on the hutch she'd painted white as a display piece—

The teapots had to go, if these first two customers were any clue. Maybe even her collection of antique coffee tins. Crumpled cowboy boots, a dusty old saddle and some rifles probably would have been a better decorating scheme.

She sighed as she donned a pair of disposable gloves and got to work on the omelets. Every few minutes she peeked out at Sophie, who was making little life rafts of her remaining Cheerios.

"They're gone," she announced solemnly when Beth backed through the swinging café doors to the kitchen with a steaming, fragrant plate in each hand.

"You can certainly have more," Beth said. "Just wait a sec—"

But then she followed Sophie's gaze to the table at the front of the café and her heart fell. A much-folded ten-dollar bill lay by each coffee cup, but the coffee had barely been touched, and the chairs were empty.

"Well, Poppin," she said on a long sigh as she put the plates down on Sophie's table. "How about having a second course?"

THE MORNING DRAGGED ON, AND ON.

Two elderly ladies came for a cup of tea.

The pharmacist strolled in at ten for coffee and a croissant to go.

She'd decided to open for just breakfast and lunch, and see how things went, but after a deserted house throughout the noon hour, she started counting the minutes until one-thirty. Maybe this whole idea had been one huge, expensive mistake. What had she been *thinking?*

And then the bells tinkled madly over the front door, and she came out of the kitchen to find Walt and Joel standing by a table, and four rugged-looking ranchers hovering just inside the door.

The smile Joel flashed at her warmed her clear to her toes.

But before she could say anything to him, Gina walked in the door, her mouth a grim line and her two chastened nephews in tow. It appeared that at least half of these customers were here under duress, but if they were satisfied, maybe the word would spread.

"This table okay?" Walt asked, tipping his head toward one in the corner.

"Anywhere—anywhere at all." She took a deep breath. "And just for today, the entrees and desserts are on the house."

# CHAPTER TEN

THE OFFER OF FREE FOOD produced a sea of smiles. But when Beth got everyone seated with menus in front of them, the smiles faded to expressions of consternation, and for Gina's two nephews, a new round of blushes.

Beth hovered at the lunch counter in back, watching them, as Joel's words marched through her thoughts.

Grits.

Corn bread.

Roadhouse barbecue.

With the exception of Walt, Joel and Gina, her patrons were rough-and-tough cowhands who'd probably never set foot in a tearoom, and until she did some décor makeovers, that's just what the place looked like. The fancy names on the menu undoubtedly compounded the problem.

These first customers were probably accomplished people in their own right, but given their expressions, they wouldn't know a *croque en bouche* from a cow pie…and weren't very eager to find out, either.

Gina met her gaze, smiled and stood up. "Okay. I promised you guys that this food is *good*. Some of the pastries might have fancy names, but it's all good, down-home cooking at its best. I know I was baffled at Starbucks at first. I had no clue how to pronounce the names of those coffee drinks, and I was too embarrassed to try. So for those of you who came here because of me, I'm coming to your tables, and we're going to talk."

Bemused, Beth relinquished her order pad, and watched Gina move around the room reading some of the names on the menu, her infectious smile and laughter setting her hulking male relatives at ease.

"We're set," Walt called out to Beth.

She crossed over to their table and took their order. "I'm sure glad you came," she murmured. "This morning looked pretty bleak."

Walt handed back his menu and smiled. "A talented girl like you will have this place hopping in no time. I just hope you'll still have time for us at the clinic."

"No problem there—late afternoon still works great for me." She leaned closer and lowered her voice to a whisper. "Though if things don't pick up fast here, I'll be more available than I want to be."

At the twinkle in Walt's eyes, she realized the double meaning of her words. "For work," she amended quickly. "At the clinic."

Walt had been dropping broad hints for weeks about her staying in town permanently, and he'd been entirely too obvious about who she ought to be dating.

She glanced at Joel, who was reading the back of the lunch menu. He'd apparently missed his uncle's subtle implication and the heated blush that had to be obvious to everyone else in the room.

She turned on her heel, went to the kitchen and started on their order, thankful that Anna had been able to pick up Sophie and watch her for the afternoon. With no servers to tend the front of the house just yet, even a small rush of customers would mean she needed to hurry along to cover all the bases herself.

Both Walt and Joel had ordered the chicken, almond and grape salad on a croissant, with a cup of lobster bisque. Donning her plastic gloves, she quickly assembled the sandwiches on her country blue stoneware plates, and ladled the bisque into matching soup cups. She added a garnish of watercress and fresh strawberries on each plate, a sprig of parsley on the bisque, and made it out to the front of the house in—she glanced at the clock—three minutes flat.

Walt's ever-present, benevolent smile widened

with true appreciation when he looked down at his meal. "This smells *wonderful,* Beth."

Joel nodded, and grinned up at her. "If it tastes half as good as it looks, you're going to be over-whelmed with customers."

Warmth spread through her at his low voice and expression of frank admiration. "Steady business would be good. Overwhelmed would be even better, believe me."

His grin faded to a more somber expression. "When you have a minute, I've got a few ques-tions. I'll be at the clinic until five or so."

So he could ask her more about the past? No thanks. For the past two days their last conversation had played through her thoughts, and she didn't want to go down that road again.

The fact that Joel had delved into her past still felt like a violation of her privacy…even if she un-derstood the reasoning behind it. But his discover-ies were embarrassing nonetheless.

Especially in light of the physical attraction she could not dispel.

The irony was that she'd lived a goody-two-shoes life to the point of returning extra change when clerks made errors in her favor, and now words like *investigation* and *embezzlement* were never far from her thoughts.

The bell over the front door tinkled, and Loraine Gilbert strolled in. Dressed as always in her boots, well-worn jeans and a western shirt, she was the sun-browned image of a strong ranch woman from her assured air to her businesslike stride.

But when her gaze drifted to Joel and Walt's table, her stride faltered. What Beth had already suspected surely had to be true—the woman had a thing for Walt, whether he knew it or not.

And maybe the two of them could use a little help.

"I'm so glad you stopped in, Ms. Gilbert." Beth directed her to a table adjacent to Walt's and handed her a menu. Just as Beth hoped, Walt stood and pulled back a chair for her at his own table. "The special today is a good one—anything you see, on the house."

Loraine gave the menu a brief, decisive glance and handed it back. "The fresh fruit and crab salad plate. Brioche. Black coffee. Thanks."

Walt laughed. "That's my Lorrie. Never dithered a day in her life."

"Once," she retorted. "And that taught me a lesson I never forgot."

Wishing she could stay and listen to their usual banter, Beth headed back in the kitchen and started Loraine's plate.

Gina walked in a moment later with four order tickets in her hand. She blew at her bangs. "I swear, you'd think those cowboys had never stepped foot off the ranch. Took forever and a day to get this down for you."

Over Gina's shoulder and the top of the swinging café doors, Beth could see the men chuckling and elbowing each other. "Or they were having fun with you."

She followed Beth's gaze, then rolled her eyes. "Auntie Gina is not pleased if that's the case. So, how are you going to handle serving *and* cooking?"

"Soups, stews and casserole specials will all be made ahead, of course. The sandwich selection will vary each day, but each is quick to assemble."

"Good plan." Gina looked at her watch. "Oops, I need to get back to school for a meeting. If you have any trouble with those bozos, be sure to let me know." She winked. "They may all act like John Wayne, but they are marshmallows inside. Believe me."

"But you haven't had anything to eat." Beth quickly assembled a pesto chicken sandwich, settled it in a clear plastic take-out box and handed it to her. "At least take this. And dessert—"

"Better not go that far. I know it would be delicious. I'd be addicted. And then I'd be here every single day." Gina patted her hips. "But thanks a million for the sandwich."

With a quick hug, she disappeared through the swinging doors.

A deep feeling of contentment welled up in Beth's heart as she prepared and served her first customers.

A business of her own.

Growing friendships.

After years of frequent moves and little time or opportunity to develop relationships with other women, it all seemed so perfect....

The phone rang. And for once, the ring didn't make her heart skip a beat. Perhaps this would be a take-out order from yet another one of Gina's obedient relatives, or even from someone else.

She picked up the phone, and imagined the caller could hear the happiness in her voice when she said, "Crystal's Café, can I help you?"

But it wasn't the unfamiliar voice of a new customer on the line, and the caller didn't waste time saying hello.

"*Beth.*" Anna Garcia's voice trembled. "I brought Sophie inside right away, and I—I called the sheriff."

Beth drew in a sharp breath as a thousand scenarios raced through her thoughts. "Is she hurt? What happened?"

"Th-there was a car. And a man. I was outside with the kids, and I didn't see him right away. Then one of the boys said he was *watching* us." Anna's voice shook. "But when I turned, I knew it wasn't all of us. He was focused on Sophie, Beth. And he was so intent that he didn't realize I'd noticed him. When he saw me, he got in the car and roared away."

An icy chill swept through Beth. *Sophie.* "Th-the sheriff?"

"Not here yet. His offices are in the middle of the

county. I—I know this could just be my imagination, but I swear, that man was staring at her—and if I hadn't been outside with the kids…"

Beth leaned her forehead against the wall, fighting back the fear that had dogged her night and day during those last weeks in Chicago.

The threat had been very real there, too.

There'd been the anonymous phone calls.

The sense of being watched.

One night, someone broke into her house while she and Sophie were away, and trashed the den Patrick had used as his home office.

And then a few weeks later it happened again… with much greater repercussions.

"I'm on my way, Anna. Five minutes at the most."

She scooped a variety of pastries and desserts on a platter, pocketed her car keys and took off her gingham apron. Backing through the swinging doors into the front of the house, she fixed a cheery smile on her face.

"Here you go, folks." She put the tray on a table. "Help yourself to these, and to the coffeepot. I have to leave for a bit, but I'm sure glad you came!"

She ignored their startled expressions as she hurried back to the kitchen, burst through the back door and ran for her car. Viper shot past her like an ebony blur and vaulted into the car as soon as she opened the door.

Behind her, Beth heard Joel calling her name as she

threw the SUV into gear. But nothing was more important than reaching Sophie and holding her tight…and any explanations would be a waste of time.

SOPHIE IMPATIENTLY STRUGGLED out of Beth's arms. "You're holding me too tight, Momma!"

She wanted to hold on and never, ever let go, but Beth forced herself to watch her daughter scamper across Anna's living room to the toy farm set where Olivia was playing.

Anna watched her somberly. "I didn't mean to frighten you. I…could be wrong."

Beth bit her lower lip, remembering the anonymous caller's threat at the end of April. "First instincts are usually right. Did you see the man's face?"

"I was on the other side of the yard, and he was in the shade of that big live oak in the back. I can't even be sure what kind of car he drove, because it was in the shade too, and partly hidden by the bushes along our fence. Then he took off like his tail was on fire." Anna ran a hand through her hair. "He was a big man, though. Tall and heavyset. He reminded me of Hubie—" At a sharp knock on the door, she rose from the couch and hurried to the front entry.

But it wasn't the sheriff knocking. It was Joel, and his face was taut with worry.

"Is everyone all right?" he asked, glancing between the two women and the children playing quietly on the floor.

Anna silently stepped aside to let him in and darted a glance at Beth, clearly leaving any explanations to her.

"Thanks to Anna," Beth said quietly. "But it's probably better if she knows what's going on."

Anna raised a hand, palm up. "If this is private, you really don't need to say anything."

"My husband may have been in some legal trouble before he died. Afterward, someone stalked me in Chicago, and threatened to follow me here." Beth swallowed. "I've had some hang-up calls, and that vandalism at the café. I have no idea if it's all related, or not."

Joel frowned at Anna. "Have you called the sheriff?"

She nodded. "But he said it might be an hour. I can't imagine what we'd do in a real emergency. We're at the edge of the county, and response times are usually real slow."

Her gaze veered toward the other children, and Beth knew she had to be worried about the safety of all of them. "I'm thinking that I should probably keep Sophie home with me for a while."

Anna's eyes flared wider. "I don't want you to think—"

"I know you'd keep Sophie safe, believe me. But it's too much to ask right now, when you've got other little ones to watch over."

"I want to help you out. I really do…." But the

doubt and worry on Anna's face belied her words, and Beth didn't blame her a bit.

"When I know things are okay, I'll bring her back. I promise."

Joel hunkered down and beckoned for Sophie, then swept her up in his arms. It was a reflex, born of a male instinct to protect any small and defenseless child—but the soft, trusting warmth of her nearly stopped his heart. He wanted to hold her tight. Savor the scent of her shampoo, and imagine his own daughter at this age, full of life and energy—

Shaken, he turned and abruptly handed her to Beth. "Let's go back to the café. After Anna talks to the sheriff, she can send him over there. Is that okay?"

"Of course." Anna directed a worried frown at Beth. "You take care now, you hear?"

Joel gave her an easy smile. "This is probably nothing at all to worry about. But, like Beth said, it's probably better for all of you if Sophie stays home for a while. No sense borrowing trouble, right?"

Beth drew in a breath. "Oh, my—I forgot about the cash register."

"Ole Walt is guarding it," Joel said with a hint of laughter. "But that might not be a good thing. I think he's pretty casual about making change."

HE'D TRIED TO CALM their worries, and put Anna and Beth at ease. But all the way back to the café Joel's mind had raced with the very real possibility that someone might have been on the verge of abducting Sophie. The guy had certainly displayed an unusual, eerie interest in her that didn't bode well.

Sophie was one very lucky girl, but that luck might not hold out.

Beth latched the front yard gate after they went through, then locked the café's front door once they were inside.

Walt, casually seated at a table and still talking to Loraine, waved a hand toward the rest of the café. "Your customers left well satisfied," he said with a smile. "You'll notice that not one of your delightful treats is left. They didn't actually pay, but I think you've got some pretty impressive tips laying on the tables."

"I—I told them it was on the house." Beth took Sophie from Joel's arms and gave her a kiss, then put her down and knelt in front of her. "Remember what we talked about?"

Sophie nodded, her expression somber. "I stay in the house. Except if you go with me."

"Right. And if you're outside?"

"I only go if you're with me, and I stay in the yard."

"Good girl."

Sophie worried at her lower lip. "Can I go upstairs and get my dolly?"

"Of course. And we need to take Viper outside, too, so I'll come along." Beth followed her to the

stairway door at the end of the lunch counter, but
hesitated and looked back at Joel over her shoulder.
"Thanks. For *everything*."

"Anytime."

Walt cleared his throat. "Mind if I ask what's
going on?"

Loraine put her coffee cup down and pushed
away from the table. "I'll let you two talk. I need
to get my feed loaded and get back home before the
horseshoer shows up."

Joel waited until Loraine left before answering
his uncle. "It's about Sophie. There was—"

Little footsteps clattered down the stairs, and
Sophie appeared at the end of the lunch counter, her
face flushed. "My mommy doesn't feel good. She
said you should come!"

## CHAPTER ELEVEN

JOEL MOTIONED for Walt to take Sophie, then rushed up the stairs, his heart lodged in his throat. Beth didn't *feel* well? She'd been fine minutes before, but the possibilities were endless.

He'd been recertified in CPR and First Aid less than a year ago, and he'd certainly tended his share of heart attacks, strokes and other sudden in-home tragedies. He reached the upstairs landing with Walt close on his heels.

And came face-to-face with Beth.

She was standing, but shaky, her face ghost-white. Viper ricocheted from one end of the apartment to the other, growling and sniffing the floor.

"Someone was here." Her voice was monotone with shock. "I wasn't even gone an hour, and there were even customers downstairs."

"You're sure?" He rested his hands on her shoulders, half expecting her to sink to the floor, but she stiffened and pulled back.

"Th-the bedroom. Someone took a cardboard

box from the closet. It's on my bed and I can tell he went through it."

"What was in it?"

"Papers, mostly...but he also did this." She looked down at a fragile china ballerina figurine laying in pieces at her feet. "I always kept it on a high shelf, because it was my grandmother's. How could anyone know that it meant so much to me?"

"Maybe it was coincidental."

Her eyes widened as she scanned the room. "And how could someone get up here in broad daylight?"

He mentally reviewed the layout of the main floor. "None of the windows in the café face the rear. If the customers were talking, they might not have heard footsteps...or might've assumed it was just you coming back."

She shuddered. "Sophie and I could have been up here."

"He probably watched for you to leave, Beth. He must have, to use such a short window of time."

Her eyes widened. "Which means he was the person who was watching Sophie."

"Maybe. Or maybe he's been watching this place for a long time...and grew impatient enough to take a big risk. Did you lock the doors when you left?"

"Of course I did." She managed a tremulous smile. "I'm from a city, remember? That reflex comes natural as breathing."

Joel ran a hand over the door frame at the top of

the stairs, then jogged downstairs to check the rear entry. When he returned, he found her cradling the china figure in her hands. "There's no sign of the doors or windows being jimmied."

She looked at him helplessly. "So what does that mean?"

"Your friend may have slipped in another time, and found a set of keys. Or, he's a real pro at picking locks. Which means he can easily come right back."

She'd been pale before, but now she turned white as the shattered figurine. Her eyes looked huge and stricken.

"You've mentioned seeing a car lingering outside late at night."

She nodded. "S-several times. I couldn't ever see the make and model, though. Once I flipped on all the lights, turned on the porch light and threw open the front door, just to see what would happen. The guy took off like a rocket."

"I don't think you and Sophie should stay here anymore."

"But this is where we live. We have to be here…until I can get it listed and sold. I can't afford anything else."

"Any friends you could stay with?"

She closed her eyes in thought, then her shoulders sagged in defeat. She slowly shook her head.

"Gina?"

"She's divorced. She has a small place and there's no room."

"Anna?"

"How can I endanger *either* of those women and their children? Neither one of them has a husband for protection—" She seemed to catch herself. "Not that having one always makes any difference."

She was right about bringing trouble into a defenseless situation, which was why Walt's place wouldn't be a good option. And that left…

"My place." At Beth's shocked expression, he said, "I know. I'm fifteen miles out, and it's a long drive." *Though I find you way too attractive…and seeing Sophie morning and night will probably bring the old nightmares back a hundredfold.*

But it was the safest possible option, and he couldn't let her say no.

"I—I don't think so. Not that I don't appreciate the offer," she added quickly. "It's kind of you, really, but I know we'd just be in your way."

He could almost see the wheels spinning in her brain as she scrambled for good reasons to refuse.

She brightened, then added, "I'll just install extra good locks, on every window and door. I can leave the stairway door open, so Viper can patrol upstairs and down…and I could even padlock all the yard gates."

"Any guy over five feet tall could easily vault over that fence," Joel retorted.

"But the dog—"

"What if this guy has a gun? Or has dog-repellant spray? Or happens to toss poison-laced steak into your yard?"

"The locks…"

"Look around when you go downstairs, Beth. Look at all the glass windows that could be broken. And think about how long it takes for the sheriff to get here—we're way out of easy range for him and his deputies in this county."

"My café," she said, her voice laden with sadness. "The early morning hours when I need to bake. Sophie."

He knew he should offer to bring Sophie to Beth in town at a decent hour in the morning, so the little girl could sleep longer. But the thought sent a rush of unreasonable fear straight down his spine, followed by the terrible memories of trying to awaken his own little girl….

Her soft, pliant skin had felt like ice beneath his fingertips. Too firm, too still. And he'd been far too late to save her.

*What the hell did he know about little kids?* The thought terrified him.

And now, he took the easy way out, even as he silently berated himself for being every kind of fool. "You just opened today. Adjust your hours. You could open at ten or eleven. Build up your noon trade, then add some mornings later on."

"Or I could find someone to stay here at night.

Someone to hire," she added quickly. "I'm not suggesting that you'd want to do it, of course. You've got livestock and your dog at home."

She'd quickly dismissed the idea of him staying here, but now an image flashed into his thoughts— long, sultry nights. Temptation. Deeper involvement wasn't a good idea, but it was one that had grown more appealing with each passing week.

He cleared his throat, trying to erase the images that followed—of some other man staying here with Beth. Alone.

His blood pressure kicked up a notch. "So where would this person stay? State health codes won't allow someone to live in a café, and you're pretty cramped up here as it is. There'd be no privacy."

She tapped a forefinger against her lower lip. "A night watchman, maybe."

"That would cost you ten, twelve dollars an hour, easily. Multiply that by seven days a week…"

"Guess that's not such a good plan."

"Or, you could stay in the country with me for a while, until we have some answers. I don't think you'll sleep well at night if you stay here." He knew she wouldn't like the next part, but this time he would be up front. "In the meantime, we could work on a security system, and try to get the sheriff actively working on this situation. So far, he's been useless. And, we can start looking into your husband's past. Maybe there'll be some clues pointing to the guy who has been harassing you."

She sank back in her chair with weary acceptance. "You're right, of course. I'm...grateful for your offer."

"Good, then. Let's check over this place, inch by inch, so you can see if anything is missing, and then we'll get you two and the dog packed and ready to go. You could put a sign in the window saying you'll be opening at eleven or so. Deal?"

A suspicion of tears glistened in her eyes as she surveyed her apartment, but then she swallowed hard and lifted her chin, her hands clenched at her sides. "Definitely a deal. And I promise to pay you for everything you do."

"It's not about money, Beth. Not that at all. It's about keeping you and your little girl safe."

Beth had seemed shell-shocked at the violation of her home, yet she'd quickly rallied. He could see her determination in the set of her shoulders and the glint in her eyes.

A familiar warmth crept back into his chest... one that had grown stronger every day that they'd worked side by side. One that reminded him that he'd been fooling himself almost from the start.

Initially, he'd told himself that he needed to stay close enough to Beth to find out if she'd be a trust-worthy employee for Walt. Maybe it had been a rea-sonable concern, but it sure hadn't taken long to find out that his doubts had been misplaced.

The death of his daughter and his bitter divorce had been hard lessons, and he knew he couldn't ever face that kind of commitment again. Yet he was bringing Beth and Sophie into his home.

How was he going to keep his distance now?

AFTER THOROUGHLY GOING through the apartment with her, Joel helped Beth with the cleanup of the café and some prep work for tomorrow. The sun was low in the sky when she finally buckled Sophie into her car seat and followed him out of town. The narrow two-lane highway wound past several deep ravines, then shot straight as an arrow toward the setting sun, deep into ranch country.

Endless miles of barbed-wire fence flanked the highway on both sides, broken only by an occasional gate protected by a cattle guard, or a ranch sign suspended over a lane that disappeared into the rolling hills without a house, barn or human in sight.

While Sophie dozed in the backseat, Beth had entirely too much time to think…and to second-guess her decision to accept his generous offer.

She'd already known Joel was an honorable man. A protector, who put his family above all else. She'd seen it in the way he'd guarded Walt's interests, by being cautious about her. In the way he'd paid exquisite attention to the smallest details in the renovations at the clinic, going well beyond what Walt had asked for.

He was a good man. His quiet sense of humor and his strength touched her heart. But the thought of staying at his home gave her a shiver of apprehension.

She had no doubt about his intentions. No doubt that he would be honorable in this situation, too, and not take advantage of the isolation and her vulnerability. What she doubted was herself.

Dusky, quiet evenings.

Long, dark nights.

Staying with someone who stirred her emotions and desires more than Patrick ever had, even in the earliest days of their marriage. What on earth had she been thinking, agreeing to follow Joel to his secluded home?

The western sky was a brilliant palette of violets, indigo and deep rose when his taillights finally glowed red and his blinker signaled a left-hand turn onto a narrow gravel road.

Rolling down her window, she breathed in a faint hint of cattle and horses. She cautiously followed him down a rutted lane that wound through low rolling hills dotted with mesquite and prickly pear. The lane dropped into a thick stand of trees, and now the air bore the fresh, moist scent of a nearby creek. Ahead, she could make out a long, single-story house set deep in the shadows.

She parked next to his truck and took Sophie out of her car seat, resting the sleeping child against her shoulder. Joel pulled the dog carrier out of the back, opened it and snapped a leash on Viper's collar.

"This is lovely," she murmured. "How on earth did you ever find this place?"

"By chance." He led the way up the flagstone walk to the front door. "It was an Internet listing. It said 'isolated' and that appealed to me, after living in the city for so long." He flipped on the lights, then ushered her through the front door. "I may have gone a bit overboard on the isolation part, but the place suits me. Cattle, a few horses and a dog are more than enough company on most days."

Knowing that he'd been a near recluse for months after moving to Texas and that he still lived alone, she'd expected to find a bare-bones house devoid of warmth and personality, but with bachelor clutter and dust.

It was anything but.

The entry opened into a spacious great room paneled in oak, with a massive fieldstone fireplace filling most of one wall. To the left, a wide archway opened into a long hall that probably led to the bedrooms, while to the right, another led into a large kitchen with terra-cotta flooring.

The oversize leather furniture in the living area looked marshmallow soft and inviting, while the wildlife prints on the walls completed the masculine, yet warmly inviting atmosphere.

And not one thing was out of place.

Even the massive bloodhound mix, curled up in front of the fireplace, appeared to be perfectly arranged. He raised his head, his attention fixed on Viper. "A-roo-ooo," he warbled in apparent greeting.

He sounded like a yodeler with laryngitis, and Viper was not impressed. She rushed to the end of her leash and stiffened to full attention, issuing a make-my-day growl that promised she wouldn't be taking any prisoners.

The bloodhound's chin dropped to the floor and his eyes closed.

"Oh, dear," Beth murmured.

"He thinks she's a nightmare. When he wakes up, they'll be fine." The old dog started snoring. "Though that probably won't be anytime soon. Earl needs his naps."

Beth laughed. "I'm sure he's a great watchdog for you. This is a lovely place!"

Joel shrugged. "It was once a working ranch, but then this part was divided off, and developed as a hunting lease operation. After the owner died, his kids fought over it for a while, then put it up for sale. They left it as is—furnishings, linens and even the kitchen equipment. There's a cabin that bunks six hunters."

"Wow." It was such a cliché, and yet, the only word she could find. "What do people hunt around here?"

"Deer. Turkey. Quail. The owner had it in a game management program." He headed down the hallway to the left, leading the way past a bedroom that was probably his, past several more doors, and then through a doorway that opened into another short hallway to the right. "This part was for hunters," he said. "Three bedrooms and a private bath, and the hall door locks from the inside."

He showed her into the first bedroom. It was spartan, with taupe walls and mission oak furnishings, but the hobnail lamp cast a soft glow and made the art print of deer on the wall seem to come alive.

Beth settled Sophie in the middle of the queen-sized bed. "This is really so kind of you," she whispered.

He tipped his head in acknowledgment. "No problem. I'm afraid this part of the house hasn't been dusted in weeks, though. I have a local cleaning lady come out once a month, but that's about it. I'll call her tomorrow and see if she can fit in another trip."

"Please don't," Beth said quickly, touched by his thoughtfulness. "I'd be more than happy to do it—and the rest of the place, too. I owe you. In fact—this place was set up for paying guests, and I really should be paying you. Just tell me—"

"No. It's no big deal—just a short-term favor for a friend." He turned and headed out into the hallway. "I'll bring in your things, so you can stay here. Sophie might be frightened if she awakens in a strange place."

Beth sank into a rocker in the corner of the room, watching the gentle rise and fall of the soft old quilt with Sophie's breathing, as Joel's footsteps faded away. Feeling as safe and warm and protected as her child, for the first time since the car accident. She'd found good friends and thoughtful people here. A decent place to stay.

But still, someone had come to Texas.

Someone who was after a nonexistent key and documents she could not find.

Someone who wanted to frighten her, and might not stop at that.

And now, the all-too familiar litany of her sleepless nights began to pulse through her thoughts. *Oh, Patrick…what did you do?*

## CHAPTER TWELVE

BETH ADJUSTED Sophie's covers, then stepped out of the bedroom, leaving the door ajar and the hall light on. She found Joel in the kitchen, making a pot of coffee.

"Decaf?" he asked. "Otherwise, there's tea."

"Sweet or northerner?"

"After fifteen years in Detroit?"

"Tea." She managed a weary smile. "I'm not up to speed on Texas sweet tea yet, either." She guessed at the cupboard to the right of the sink. "Glasses?"

Leaning a hip against the kitchen counter, he nodded. "Is Sophie all right?"

"Exhausted. She usually doesn't go to sleep this early." Beth filled her glass with ice from the dispenser in the refrigerator door, then poured herself a glass of tea from the gallon jug inside. "I can't thank you enough for your hospitality."

"Not a problem."

She suddenly felt more than a little exhausted

herself. Late in the afternoon, the sheriff had stopped at Anna's house, took her statement, and then he'd come over to the café. Without a license plate, make of car, or physical description of the man, there'd been little to go on.

Still, he'd promised that a deputy would swing past the café every night during the coming week, barring call-outs to other parts of the county.

She looked around, suddenly aware of the unusual silence without the constant clickety-click of Viper's toenails. The dog never, ever seemed to sit still. "Did Earl eat my dog?"

Joel laughed. "Earl is in *love*." He nodded toward the sliding glass doors opening out onto a patio illuminated by several old-fashioned gas lamps. "Viper's patrolling the perimeter of the yard like a miniature marine, and he's watching her with total adoration. Most exercise he's had in a week."

Beth peered outside. Sure enough, she could see a little black form marching along the fence. Earl had parked himself on the patio, and was swiveling his head as he watched her go back and forth.

"Those are Earl's aerobics," Joel added solemnly. "He does them so fast that you can barely see him move."

She'd felt uncertain and a little awkward, coming out to this isolated place with a man she hadn't known long, but now she felt some of that tension ease. Any man with a dog like Earl just had to be a decent guy.

"So, how're you doing?"

"This was quite a day. From the excitement of opening the café, to taking refuge because…" She shuddered. "It's so creepy, thinking that someone was in my house, going through my things. What if Sophie and I had been home?"

"I'd guess your intruder was careful to make sure that didn't happen. He's probably been watching for some time, trying to make sure you wouldn't be around."

"Somehow, that doesn't make me feel a whole lot better." Beth took a long, slow swallow of tea, thankful for the cool, smooth slide of it down her parched throat. "And the sheriff wasn't very reassuring, either. At least he's going to be asking some questions around town, though. One possibility was that vagrant—Hubie Post."

"From what I hear, Hubie has a checkered past."

"Which opens up a whole new realm of possibilities, and even more worries." She shuddered. "His name came up after my place was trashed, though Talbot said he hasn't seen Hubie in the area for months."

She paused, considering. Talbot had said Hubie was a loner, an ongoing casualty of Vietnam who'd never held a long-term job and who spent his Social Security checks at the local taverns. He'd racked up considerable time in the county lockup over the years—mostly for bar fights and public intoxication. But he'd never been charged with vandalism or a violent crime, and he wasn't on the sex offender list, either. *Yet.*

"There's no proof that he was the man watching Sophie," Joel said.

"Proof or not, you can bet he isn't coming within a hundred feet of my daughter. Ever." Beth held out her hands, palms up. "But if he *was* the guy who was watching her, is he also the one who went through my things?" She managed a dry laugh. "On *CSI,* there'd be a big interrogation and they'd dust my entire place for prints. We'd have answers in an hour—including commercials."

"They always get their lab results right away, too." A corner of Joel's mouth lifted. "At least Talbot and his deputies will be keeping a closer eye on things." He refilled her glass of tea, then poured himself a cup of coffee. "If they see him, they'll pick him up for questioning."

"I have my doubts about him, though. Why would a total stranger target me? It makes no sense."

"Which leaves the only other real suspect—the guy in Chicago. Your husband left you quite a legacy."

"I still can't believe he was capable of theft." Beth stared at the inky darkness beyond the windows. "Can you imagine living with someone, and then wondering if you ever really knew him?

Patrick had a good job. He supported us well. Why risk everything for a single windfall?"

"True. But if he didn't, why would anyone be so persistent now?"

She snorted. "And I cannot imagine who would've chosen Patrick for a partner in crime. You have no idea just how quiet and unassuming he was."

"Try to think back—anything unusual about his connections to friends? Neighbors? Anyone he might've mentioned during his last few months?"

The aroma of the coffee made her stomach growl, and she folded her arms around her stomach. "Believe me, I want answers, too, but nothing really adds up."

"Why?"

"We barely knew our new neighbors. It was difficult to socialize with old friends because Pat worked such long hours. And he wasn't the kind of guy who met buddies for a beer after work, either."

"What about his boss?"

"Roger Bennings is the owner of the company. That man was livid about the loss of all that money." She suppressed a shudder. "After the police finished investigating, he called me two or three times. He sure wasn't polite."

A muscle ticked along Joel's lean jaw. "I'd say that was harassment."

"Desperation, was more like it." Even now, she could hear the note of simmering anger in Roger's voice, edged with a hint of fear. The losses had been large enough to endanger the future of his company. "But what could I say?"

Joel frowned. "Do you think he could've been desperate enough to take things a step further?"

"He wasn't my crank caller, if that's what you mean. I'd recognize Roger's gravelly voice anywhere." Beth paused. Thought back. "And he isn't the type, anyway. He has to be seventy by now. He would hire a P.I. or an attorney, not some lowlife. Patrick once said that Roger didn't hesitate to file lawsuits over business deals."

"Was he your husband's direct boss?"

"Nope. Ewen Farley, who's a strict, no-nonsense guy. We had him and his wife over for dinner a couple of times, but we were never close. Ewen was mortified about the disappearance of all that money, right from under his nose. Probably afraid he'd lose his job."

"Was he questioned?"

Beth nodded. "At length. Everyone at the company was, or so I heard. Ewen and his wife stopped over with their condolences after Pat died and they came to the funeral, but they were both really distant. I could tell they still thought Pat was responsible and probably figured I was involved, too."

"Did they say anything?"

"Not in so many words." She closed her eyes briefly against the memory of those awkward encounters. When they'd come by her house, they'd murmured sympathetic words, but they'd both surreptitiously glanced around her entryway and living room, as if somehow expecting to see new, state-of-the-art electronics or priceless artwork crowded into every corner.

"What about secretaries or bookkeepers—did Patrick ever mention someone in particular?"

Beth sorted through her memories and came up dry. "He was never the schmoozing type." She twisted the simple wedding band she'd moved to her right hand. "He always kept his sights on leaving that job and opening his own accounting firm someday."

"Any number of other employees could've taken the money, over time."

"That's what I've always thought."

"And when Patrick died, they would've had a perfect place to lay the blame."

"A man who could hardly defend himself."

"But then the question is, what would this person be after now? Since he got off scot-free so far, why risk raising suspicions—or the chance of being caught?"

"My caller mentioned a key and some documents, but I went through all of Patrick's home office files before moving here. *Everything.* If there was anything incriminating, I sure didn't see it…and I certainly never found a suspicious-looking key." Beth hesitated, knowing that telling Joel any more would just sow more seeds of doubt about her past. "There was a break-in and fire at my house in Chicago just weeks after the funeral. We weren't home, but the neighbors smelled smoke and called 911."

"Arson?" Joel shoved a hand through his hair.

"Definitely. And the cops, fire marshal and insurance investigator all suspected me." She gave a bitter laugh. "They thought it convenient that Sophie and I had just left town to visit relatives. And, they were rather curious about a widow in financial straits coming so close to losing her house and gaining a tidy insurance settlement."

"Was it obvious that someone else had been in the house?"

She met and held his gaze, but saw only compassion in his eyes. "A few things were disarrayed in Pat's home office. There were minor screwdriver marks on an unlocked window, where someone had managed to pry it open. The rest of the house was perfect. I think the cops thought I'd done it, but they couldn't prove anything. I was never charged."

"Which is why there was nothing in the newspaper archives."

"There was more smoke than fire damage, so it wasn't headline news by any means. Minor incidents are listed in the fire-and-police log section of the paper by street address, so a search of the archives wouldn't have turned up anything under our name."

"So…moving here wasn't just about your aunt's property."

She felt her shoulders sag. "I couldn't afford the huge mortgage payments on my old house, so I listed it as soon as the fire damage was repaired. But it sold for far less than it was worth, and most of the money went to settle bills."

He nodded. "A tough situation to be in."

"Now part of me loves this place so much that I want to stay. But if I did, I'd have to buy out my sister's share." She drew in a slow breath. "And— with everything that's happened here, I feel like I should grab Sophie and run."

"You're safe now," Joel said quietly.

"Because we're taking advantage of your hospitality by hiding like frightened rabbits. How long can we do that?"

"You've been here just a couple hours, and you certainly haven't worn out your welcome," he said mildly. When her stomach growled again, he added, "Hungry? I'm not much of a cook, but I can throw an omelet together, or make some sandwiches."

When she hesitated, he lifted a cast-iron skillet from the cupboard. "I'll take that as a yes."

It did funny things to her insides, watching him capably sort through the herbs in his spice cabinet and start pulling ingredients out of the refrigerator.

A green pepper. A basket of fresh mushrooms,

eggs and sharp cheddar. From a wire basket on the counter he gathered an onion and fresh garlic.

Patrick had never shown any interest in the kitchen, preferring to leave all of that up to her, but there was something innately sexy in this man's easy confidence, whether he was wielding a hammer or cracking fresh eggs one-handed over a crockery bowl.

"Not much of a cook, you said," she murmured, watching the flash of his knife as he expertly diced and sautéed the veggies. "I'd say you know your way around a kitchen pretty well."

"My parents owned a restaurant, so I put in plenty of hours during high school." He rolled his eyes. "Believe me, working under an authoritarian father and a chef with a Napoleon complex pretty much cured me of any desire to stay in the family business."

"No wonder you had such great ideas for the layout of my café," she teased.

He grabbed a couple of earth-tone rattan place mats from a drawer, set them with two place settings of bronze-and-copper glazed stoneware plates, and served the omelets with thick slices of dark Russian rye spread with butter. "My cleaning lady brings me the bread," he said with a smile. "She's sure that I must be starving, since I live alone."

The omelets were perfect—fragrant with the

onion and garlic and chunks of honey-glazed ham, the bread a perfect contrast. Beth closed her eyes, savoring the first bite. "I didn't realize I was hungry until now. This is sheer bliss."

"Thanks. Basic stuff, though. I've never tackled the kind of pastries you made for the café." The laugh lines at the corners of his eyes deepened. "Those cowhands had no idea just how special your food is."

She paused, her fork in the air. "But you were right, you know. Serving the wrong menu probably confounded every one of the guys who showed up today. They were looking for something down-home and filling, not fancy. I'll be lucky if any of them come back…and when the word spreads, no one else will show up, either."

"I wouldn't be so sure." Joel finished off his coffee and went over to the pot to refill his cup, then topped off Beth's glass of tea. "I called Walt on the way over here. He's been talking up your place to every one of his clients. Loraine is at it, too."

She'd felt edgy for hours. At the thought of the kindness of so many people in this small town, she felt her eyes start to burn. "That's so nice of them. Really."

"It's just what people do around here—help out, if they can." He saluted her with his coffee cup. "And believe me, ordering food at the bars in town is just asking for trouble. Your place will catch on in a hurry."

*But not everyone is optimistic.* Beth's appetite faded. "Do you know anything about the restaurant in Horseshoe Falls? The woman who owns it once told me that Crystal's didn't have a chance."

"Well, she's wrong." He took his plate to the sink, rinsed it and dropped it into the dishwasher. "Walt says that other place went belly-up a couple times in the past, and it's struggling this time around, too."

Beth idly pushed a section of omelet to one side of her plate. "I suppose that would explain her attitude."

"Want to scope out the competition?"

She looked up, startled. "What?"

He smiled. "We could run over there for supper sometime. Your café closes by early afternoon, anyway. What about Friday?"

"Well…" She felt herself starting to flounder. It wouldn't be a date, of course, just a quick dinner with a friend. Yet, it was getting harder to stay behind that line of simple friendship, because Joel had become so much more than simply a man she'd contracted for renovations.

They'd both kept a careful, cautious distance since the dance. Yet, with each passing day, she saw something new and deeper in him that drew her at the most elemental level. She knew, without doubt, that he was a man she could trust…with her heart, and with her life.

Which made it all the more important to keep those barriers in place.

"This would not be a date," he added dryly. "In case you're worried. You could consider it covert market research. If that place is having trouble getting established, we can do a comparison study and see what you should be doing differently at Crystal's."

She dissolved in helpless laughter. "Then by all means, we'd better go."

THE FOLLOWING MORNING, Joel sighed as he finished installing the final dead-bolt lock set on the front and back doors of the house, and stepped back to assess his handiwork.

The doors were all solid-core oak. Coupled with two-inch bolts of case-hardened steel and oversized strike plates, it would take a determined burglar to get through them. The old-fashioned windows were a different story. They were each a good six feet tall, and could be easily breached by breaking the glass.

Beth stepped out of the café's kitchen, wearing a flour-dusted apron. She'd arranged a play corner for Sophie, with a bright red rug, child-size table and chairs and a chest overflowing with toys. Now, she set a glass of milk and a sandwich on the table and settled Sophie in her chair with a hug and a kiss.

The sheer Norman Rockwell domesticity of it all never failed to touch the empty places in Joel's heart. He turned away sharply, and busied himself with collecting his tools.

"So, how's it going?" Beth called out. She came

across the room and bent to study the gleaming brass interior handle. "Mmmm...I love that old-fashioned look. Fits in perfectly with this place."

"The most important thing is that they're stronger than what you had." He tipped his head toward the six double-hung windows facing the street. "You've also got better locks on them, but they're still a weak point."

"The security system people called this morning. They're scheduled to come in two weeks."

Joel hefted his toolbox and opened the door. "A good thing. But the value is contingent on the ability of the cops to show up, and we both know how long the response time is around here."

"Still..."

"Still, you've got new keys, in case that guy had an old one. Your security system signs and emblems in the windows might be a deterrent. And, you have a safe place to stay at any rate."

She touched his arm as he started out the door. A light touch that barely brushed his shirt, yet it made him stop dead in his tracks and sent a rush of warmth to places that had absolutely no business showing any sort of interest in a woman who simply needed his help and nothing more.

"I want to thank you, and I'm not sure if I've let you know how much this means to me."

He turned and looked down into blue, blue eyes that held a suspicious sheen of moisture, even though he knew she was one tough lady who held her emotions in check. "No problem," he said gruffly.

She hesitated, then wrapped her arms around his neck and gave him a swift kiss on the cheek. "I can't tell you how good it is to feel safe…after such a long, long time."

Bemused, he watched her pivot and disappear into the kitchen. It took another minute for him to gather his thoughts and go out the door. *Safe?*

He'd do his damned best to keep her and the little girl safe from whoever was threatening them with harm.

But could he keep her safe from himself?

## CHAPTER THIRTEEN

FRIDAY NOON BROUGHT in two retired schoolteachers, the banker and a potbellied trucker who was passing through town, Walt noticed with satisfaction as he took the same table he'd had for three days in a row.

Beth straightened her red-and-white checked apron and strolled over to Walt's table with a smile. "Glad to see you back again."

He pointed out the lunch special of the day, a Reuben, deli slaw and homemade chicken barley soup. "Can't stay away," he announced, loud enough for residents in the next county to hear. "Never had food good as this, anywhere."

The trucker glanced at him over the top of his menu, then went back to reading it, his brow furrowed. "I'm hungry for a half-pound burger 'n' onion rings," he muttered when Beth came to his table. "Where's the real food on this thing?"

"You come through this area often?" Beth asked.

"Every week or so. Why?"

She tipped her head and smiled. "We just opened, and I'll consider this an investment in you. I'd recommend what Dr. Walt just ordered. If you aren't happy, then your lunch is on me. Either way, I'll toss in a dessert. Deal?"

His frown faded. "I'd say that's a mighty good one, sister."

Walt ground his teeth. Since her opening day, Beth had revamped the menu, adding steakhouse-style sandwiches and heartier soups to the fancy stuff, but it was still going to be an uphill battle. The fools around here didn't realize just how good her food was—or how much that sweet little gal needed a break.

He leaned back in his chair and hooked one booted foot over his opposite knee. "Dandy place, I guarantee," he called out.

Sophie looked up from her play table in the corner where she was serving tea to her dolly, and ran over to him. "Wanna have lunch with Maisie 'n' me?"

He grinned and lifted her onto his knee. "I'd love that, squirt. But I'm expecting an old friend, and I think we're both too big for those little chairs."

"I got real tea," she wheedled, looking up into his face. "And *cookies.*"

Laughing, he tucked a strand of her hair behind her ear. "Maybe next time. If I keep eating your mama's cookies, I won't be fittin' in my jeans much longer."

"I nearly growed out of my shoes," she said with a proud smile. "*And* my purple jeans."

The bell over the door sounded, and Loraine walked in. Pretty as a yearling colt she was, with those long, lean legs and easy grace. In her faded jeans, open-collared white shirt, and heavy, squash blossom Navajo silver necklace, she could have been an art gallery owner or some pricey Realtor.... yet he knew she rode herd on a thousand cattle with just two hired hands, and no one was better help come branding and vaccination time.

Even after all these years, he felt his mouth go dry and his heart hitch a little whenever he saw her—and the darnedest thing was that it seemed to be getting worse.

Maybe he needed an adjustment of his heart meds.

"*Sophie.*" Beth made a subtle motion with her hand. Sophie glanced between Loraine and him, and reluctantly slid off his knee. "I gotta go."

He almost reached for her to come back, because having Sophie around made it easier to find something to say.

"Walt." Loraine slipped off her sunglasses and set her ivory straw Stetson crown-side down on the chair to Walt's right. She took the chair across from him.

"Lorrie." Silence lengthened as he fumbled for something else to say—feeling foolish and tongue-tied for the first time in decades.

From somewhere behind the swinging doors into

the kitchen, Walt heard Beth snort. A moment later, she bustled backward through the doors and served the trucker, then stopped at Walt's table. "So, you two," she said brightly. "Have any plans this week-end?"

She still helped out at the clinic for a few hours every afternoon, and she'd been dropping hints for the past week, encouraging Walt to make a move. Now, with a handful of words, she'd just laid the cards on the table.

But words didn't change a lifelong friendship into something different, just like that. And they didn't erase the risk of soul-deep loss, if a closer relationship faltered and failed, and destroyed what they had nurtured for decades.

"Uh…I'm moving a herd to a new summer range," Loraine said, shifting in her chair. Her gaze skated to the vicinity of Walt's face, then veered away. "What about you?"

"On call, as always."

The brief, awkward moment was past, and now her face filled with sympathy and a glint of humor. "You need a break, Walt. You're too old to keep up with all that."

"And I'd say you're—" He bit back the sort of easy reply he'd always made as a wave of deep loneliness spread through him. He had his house-keeper, who was waiting with supper before she headed home to her own family. His dog.

And this spring, he'd had Joel. But at the end of the day, it was always an empty house.

A house that echoed with memories so old that now they seemed as yellowed and tattered as the photo albums he kept on a shelf. There'd been a time when his wife's face had filled his thoughts, his dreams. He'd been faithful and true to her memory. But now, he sometimes had to look at those photographs to even see her clearly.

And through all the decades since his wife's death, there'd been Lorrie, whose dry humor and steadfast friendship had made those years brighter.

Maybe he'd been a fool.

He met and held Loraine's gaze. "I'd say you're right, and that it's time for us old folks to go live a little."

Her eyes flared wider, and by gosh—was that a faint blush? His heart lifted. "So what do you say, dinner this Saturday?"

"My cattle…" she protested weakly. "I've got to—"

"Hell, Lorrie." He lowered his voice. "I think we've waited long enough, don't you?"


"DECENT FRIDAY NIGHT CROWD," Joel said. He lowered his menu and surveyed the tables in the Horseshoe Falls Steak House. "So, what do you think?"

"Nice. A bit too noisy." They'd walked through the bar area, filled with lean, muscular young cowboys and young gals in tight T-shirts knotted at slim midriffs, many of them dancing to the overloud music of Strait and Keith. Back here in the restaurant area, maybe half the tables were filled. "I'd say that Crystal's Café and this place are reaching totally different market shares," she added. "Anyone who buys my café would need a bar, music and later hours to compete for this kind of clientele."

"I hope they'll keep it just as it is." He tapped his menu. "This is a commonplace Texas steak house. You have—originality."

She laughed. "So I hear, all too often. It's starting to pay off a little, though. Between Gina and Walt, I've had quite a few patrons coerced into a first visit who've come back for a second."

"And you've been open less than a week."

"Offering free food that first day was probably the reason, though."

"Don't forget all those tips people left. They liked the food, and they probably left more than the actual menu price."

"Even my trucker did." At Joel's raised eyebrow, she told him about her bargain with the trucker who'd wanted the half-pound burger and onion rings. "He actually paid for his lunch, and promised to be back with his buddies. So I guess there's hope—though every time I offer a deal, I try not to think about the whopping bill coming from my food supplier at the end of the month."

A waitress approached, and did a double take when she noticed Beth. After taking their order she scurried away.

"She must've recognized you," Joel said quietly. "Five-to-one odds that she'll pass the word about a fellow restaurateur in the house."

She must have, because a moment later Tracy appeared at their table, in a snug black silk dress, her ebony hair swept into a complicated chignon. A heavyset, balding man in a western suit stood at her elbow.

"Nice of you to come in," she said with a tight smile. "Beth Lindstrom, Joel McAllen, I'd like you to meet my husband, Peter."

"We've heard good things about your place," Beth said. "Congratulations."

"Peter's oldest son is the new manager. We're helping him get on his feet." Tracy flicked an unreadable glance at her husband. "He'll do very well here."

"Yes, indeed," Peter boomed. "Fine young man. Honest as the day is long, and he shows a lot of promise. So, you've got that little café in Lone Wolf, right?"

"She's planning to sell out this summer, honey." Tracy fluttered a hand in dismissal, then looped her arm into the crook of his elbow. "Maybe we can pick up the place and use the land for your new warehouse." She smiled down at Beth. "That would make things easier for you, wouldn't it—a quick sale?"

Beth stiffened. "Warehouse?"

"Oil well equipment—casings and such." Tracy shrugged and looked up at her husband. "I really don't know much about all of that, though."

Joel bared his teeth in a smile. "You'll both have to stop in at Crystal's for lunch sometime and say hello."

"Yes. Yes, of course." Tracy steered her husband away. "Sometime soon. Enjoy your dinner."

Beth looked down at her clenched fists and forced them to relax. "I've never done a thing to that woman, yet she either snubs me or insults me."

Joel watched Tracy and her husband make their way through the tables. "Jealousy, maybe."

"Jealousy? Over *what?* She's gorgeous, thin, and it looks like she snagged a nice, rich oilman, too."

"Ah, but you're younger." Joel winked. "Independent. And much, much prettier. I imagine trophy wives always worry a little about newer models coming along."

Beth rolled her eyes at his obvious exaggeration.

"So Miss Texas over there probably has quite a competitive streak when it comes to other women."

Now that, she could believe. "Maybe we should just head back to Lone Wolf."

"And disappoint Sophie?" Joel stood and reached

for Beth's hand. "You said she was excited about spending the evening with Gina's daughter. So, while we're waiting, want to try a little Texas two-step?"

"I...don't know."

"C'mon," he said, with a gleam in his eye. "You'll *like* it."

His voice was deep and seemed to rumble clear through her, promising that she'd like a whole lot more than just this dance. Beth hesitated, then let him lead her out onto the crowded dance floor.

As soon as she stepped into his arms, he swept her into a turn that left her breathless and laughing, and she knew going home would've been the far safer choice.

She was at eye level with his collarbone, her right hand gently held in his left, pressed close to the hard, muscular wall of his chest. She could feel the throbbing beat of the music in the floor beneath her and the plaintive words of lost love echoing in her head, until it was just the music and Joel, and everything else around her seemed to fade away.

The air between them seemed to heat and intensify with a sense of anticipation and hunger that had no place on a dance floor filled with strangers, yet she could no more pull away from his arms than she could've flown.

The music changed to something soft and seductive.

Joel tucked her head against his chest and slowed down. "Nice," he whispered, and they dropped to a slow, rocking rhythm within the press of the other couples surrounding them.

It was *too* nice. She could feel the steady beat of his heart against her cheek. The warmth of him. The wonderfully deep, secure feeling of being protected in his arms. If the music never ended, she—

Someone tapped on her shoulder, and Joel suddenly released her.

"Dinner's on the table." Their waitress gave them an I-know-what-*you'll*-be-doing-later smirk as she turned away.

Had she been that obvious? Had Joel? Although she'd been embarrassed at the town dance a month before, now she felt something different unfurling in her heart. *Hope. Longing. Desire.*

Reality came crashing back a heartbeat later.

What was she thinking, letting herself imagine a deepening relationship with anyone? She'd trusted Patrick with all her heart, and she'd never had a clue about what he'd been up to. The price of her naiveté had been her home, security and marriage. How could she ever be sure she wasn't making the same mistake twice?

AN ENDLESS RIBBON of asphalt unfolded in front of Joel's truck headlights, flat and straight, on the way back to his ranch.

"So, what did you think of the Horseshoe Falls place?" He slid a glance at her, a dimple deepening in his cheek as his teeth flashed white in the darkness. "Meet your expectations?"

Their conversation had been comfortable over dinner. Innocuous. But now, his sidelong glance sent a tingle of awareness dancing along Beth's skin, and definitely did tingly things to her toes. It took her a moment to find her voice. "It was average. Decent, unremarkable steaks. An adequate salad bar. The dinner rolls might've been from the local grocery. They weren't memorable, but they were okay."

He laughed. "Damned by faint praise."

"No, really. It was all fine," Beth said quickly, suddenly embarrassed by her own lack of grace. "I did appreciate the invitation, and I truly enjoyed having this evening out."

"This was research, remember? Don't worry about being honest." Again, she saw the white flash of his teeth when he smiled. "And just for the record, your café has that one beat all to heck. Much better food. Pleasant, wholesome ambiance. It's not one of a million steak houses that are all alike."

Beth folded her arms across her midsection. "I still don't get Tracy's comment about turning my café into a warehouse. She knows I've been working hard at bringing the place back to life, and we're certainly not competing for the same customers. Why would she say that?"

"Just a show of arrogance, maybe." He gazed pensively at the road ahead, one hand on the top curve of the steering wheel.

At the hint of bitterness in his voice, Beth twisted in her seat a few degrees and studied his resolute profile. "Sounds like the voice of experience. What happened?"

He didn't answer.

"Um…anything to do with your job in Detroit?"

His shoulder lifted almost imperceptibly.

She gave him a teasing bump with her elbow. "C'mon—I've told you more secrets than I've told anyone else. Did you have to deal with someone like Tracy?"

"Nope." He fell silent for so long that she assumed he wasn't going to say any more. "It was me."

It took a minute for his words to register. *"You?"*

"And my arrogance got someone killed."

Startled, Beth sucked in a sharp breath, and suddenly wished she hadn't asked.

"I shouldn't have been undercover, given what had just happened in my life, but I said I was the only one who could handle it." His voice held a raw edge of pain and guilt. "I insisted, and I was wrong."

The rigid set of his jaw telegraphed a message to back off. She watched a few hundred ghostly fence posts fly by on either side of the highway before she finally ignored his silent warning and listened to her heart. "What happened?"

Joel didn't respond for five long minutes, then he sighed heavily. "I didn't react fast enough... didn't see the warning signs. An informant was shot." He swore under his breath, his voice bitter. "It was a needless, tragic death."

"But you didn't pull the trigger."

"Maybe not." He leveled a hard look at her before looking back at the highway. "But I should have kept that person safe, and I didn't. So that was the end of my career."

"But that's unfair!"

"Unfair? Not when everything goes to hell, and the only one you can blame is yourself." He gave a humorless laugh. "But I didn't 'lose my career,' according to my boss. He's been calling, asking me to end my leave early and come back. It would just take something monumental for me to ever change my mind."

## CHAPTER FOURTEEN

THERE'D BEEN A MOMENT on the dance floor when Beth had fallen under Joel's spell. When she'd imagined doing a lot more than just a Texas two-step in a crowded bar.

In the dark intimacy of his pickup on the way back to his house, she'd breathed in his subtle, sensual aftershave—probably Stetson—and had been all too aware of the sheer size of him—the broad shoulders, and the bulk of his biceps. The lean, strong curve of his jaw.

But it was his past that truly touched her heart, the guilt and anger he felt over a needless death. She wondered if he knew just how much he'd revealed in the ragged edge of his voice or the bleak expression in his eyes. Ever since, she'd been mulling over his words, *I shouldn't have been undercover, given what had just happened in my life.*

She'd inadvertently opened old wounds, and since then he'd been pensive, the expressive lines of his face etched deep with old sadness. Instinct told her to just let it be. But she couldn't—not when she sensed such inestimable grief. "What happened, Joel?"

His knuckles whitened on the steering wheel.

She waited a while, then added softly, "Sometimes it helps to talk about things."

"Really." His harsh laugh sliced through the silence. "Tell me how that makes a difference."

"I…just feel really bad for you." She angled a look at him. A muscle ticked at the side of his jaw, and his mouth had settled into a grim line. "I've had a few rough times myself, when I could've used a friend."

When he finally spoke, his voice was low and raw. "Tell me how that can bring back someone you love. It can't."

He slowed and signaled for a left-hand turn. A few miles later, he slid a glance at her. "You want to know what happened? I stayed home one afternoon so my wife could run errands. Our baby daughter was napping…and never woke up."

Beth tried to speak, but the words caught in her throat.

"SIDS, the docs said. They said it wasn't anyone's fault, but I'll never believe it. I train in CPR every year. If I'd checked on her sooner, I could've saved her."

"I was terrified over SIDS when Sophie was a baby. I read a lot of studies, Joel. They all said that—"

"I don't believe them. If I hadn't put her down for a nap right then, maybe it wouldn't have happened. If I'd been in the room, I could've done something."

"Your wife—"

"Totally agreed with me. Two weeks later, she moved out. Six months later she filed for divorce."

So he'd lost his entire family, and still shouldered the entire blame. She reached over to lay a hand on his forearm, wishing she could take him in her arms and share part of his burden, but his face was a granite, resolute mask. He gently released her hold on his arm. "I figured I could just lose myself in my career, but that was yet another incredible mistake."

"But none of this was your fault."

"Please—I know you mean well. But don't demean me with platitudes, because they don't change a thing."

She recoiled, biting back a sharp reply. He was an honorable man, a strong and determined protector whose tragedies had undoubtedly rocked his deepest beliefs about himself. And no matter what she said, she knew he wouldn't accept that he wasn't to blame. "I'm so sorry, Joel," she said quietly. "About everything."

He pulled to a stop in front of Gina's house, but just sat there with a wrist draped over the top of the steering wheel. Silvery moonlight painted the lines and angles of his face in sharp relief. "I'm just not cut out for commitment—not to a woman, not a family—not even in my old career. If nothing else, I learned that much."

"But—"

"I don't mean to sound harsh, but I want you to drop this discussion. Okay?"

He was wrong, but she knew it wouldn't help to argue...at least not now. "I'll run in to get Sophie," she murmured. "I'll be right back."

AFTER THEY PICKED UP SOPHIE, they'd driven out to his place in near silence, with her daughter asleep in her car seat and Joel pensively watching the road ahead.

Once they arrived, he helped her bring Sophie inside, but then he'd disappeared into his office. Now it was after midnight, Sophie was sound asleep on her bed, and the mild headache that had started a few hours earlier was throbbing.

Beth quietly closed Sophie's door, leaving it slightly ajar, and headed for the kitchen, her path lit by ribbons of moonlight streaming through the windows.

At the door of Joel's office she paused, then pressed two fingers against the partly closed door.

The room was dark, save for the dim glow of a desk lamp and the soft, pulsing glow of the last embers in the fireplace. He sat in a high-backed chair facing the hearth, a nearly full bottle of Jim

Beam on the floor at his side and a glass of amber liquid in his hand.

"Joel?" She whispered his name, unsure if he was asleep, then stepped farther into the room.

He rolled his head against the back of the chair to look at her, weariness etched in the deep lines bracketing his mouth. "Is Sophie all right?"

"Sleeping soundly. I think she and Gina's daughter wore themselves out playing."

His brow furrowed. "What about you?"

"In search of aspirin, actually. Do you mind…"

"The cupboard above the kitchen sink." He rose smoothly and put his glass down on a stack of papers on his desk. "Hang on and I'll get it for you."

"I can do it. Really—"

"Be right back." He disappeared out into the hallway.

Curious, she turned slowly and took in the oak paneled room, with bookshelves filling two walls to the ceiling, and an expansive desk. A more intimate and cozy version of the rest of the house, it was clearly designed for a man's comfort, from the big leather desk chair to the two heavily upholstered chairs by the fireplace.

Joel returned with a bottle of aspirin, shook a couple of tablets into her hand, and gave her a glass of water. "Bad one?"

"This should catch it. I never should've had wine

with supper." She gestured toward the shelves with the glass, trying to fill a sudden, awkward silence. "Did all those books come with the house, too?" At the faint lift of his mouth, she realized how patronizing her words sounded. "I mean—you said it was furnished, and…"

He rescued her from her floundering with a half smile. "Mine, I'm afraid. I'm just glad to finally have enough space for most of them."

Another side of him she hadn't seen. The books were an eclectic mix, from classics to thrillers to coffee-table books on art, with a few shelves of Terry C. Johnston's westerns. She leaned close and trailed a finger along their spines. "I loved these."

"They make the old west and the Teton Mountains come alive, don't they?"

She rambled on for a few minutes about the books, then glanced at the clock and drew in a sharp breath. "Sorry—I'm keeping you awake, and it's late."

He shrugged off her apology. "No problem. I would've been up anyway."

He was utterly compelling in the dim light, the planes and angles of his face cast in sharp relief and his dark eyes shadowed by his long, thick lashes. Too compelling.

She pivoted toward the door. "Thanks for a lovely evening. And again, for letting Sophie and me stay here for a while."

"Beth."

He spoke her name softly, his voice warming her skin and sending her blood thrumming through her veins at the instant remembrance of dancing in his arms tonight. Did he want something more? Did she?

She looked over her shoulder. Wanting him to move forward and take her into his arms one more time.

Half-afraid that he would.

And afraid that he wouldn't, because nothing had felt as good for a long, long time, and maybe both of them could use the comfort of an embrace, if nothing else.

He held out the aspirin. "Take the bottle. You might want more later."

She accepted it, praying the warmth rising in her face wasn't visible in the darkened room... and *definitely* hoping that he hadn't read her thoughts.

Two weeks.

Just two more weeks, and the café security system would be fully installed, and then she and Sophie could move back. By then, the Realtor might even have some prospective buyers lined up, and this chapter of her life could come to a close.

The sooner the better, too—before she completely embarrassed herself over someone she could never have.

BETH PADLOCKED the backyard gates, released Viper from her travel cage and reached down to lift Sophie for a twirl in the air.

Sophie laughed and scampered off to the swing set as soon as Beth set her down. "Watch me, Momma!"

The little dog raced after her, then took a flying tour of the perimeter of the yard, barking at grass-hoppers and birds before settling down like a fierce, miniature black sphinx to watch Sophie.

It had been a full week since Beth and Joel went to the restaurant in Horseshoe Falls. A good week, in most respects.

There'd been no more problems with crank calls or other troubles.

Her noon business had been climbing steadily.

And after next week, when she and Sophie could move back to their apartment above the café, she could easily start the breakfast hours once again.

The local Realtor was busy, as well. She'd been over to take dozens of photographs, and promised the café's listing would be up on her Web site this week. Which was a very *good* thing, Beth reminded herself sharply whenever she started having doubts.

They'd come more often lately.

And now, watching Sophie swing in the shade of the massive live oak filled her with a sense of home and connectedness that she certainly hadn't felt at the pretentious house she'd just sold back in Illinois, or the overpriced house they'd owned before that one.

The apartment over the café was sweet and cozy, its windows looking out into the branches of the surrounding trees, its fanciful windows and steeply pitched ceilings adding a fairy-tale air.

And then there was Joel.

Sharing his house had been awkward at first; each of them carefully observing unseen boundaries; each of them superficially polite and distant. But in the last few days that awkwardness had faded into the easy camaraderie they shared elsewhere. She smiled to herself, remembering their conversation last night out on his porch swing.

They'd watched the stars. Listened to coyotes howl and the ghostly call of distant owls. And they'd talked until almost two in the morning about everything and nothing, until the grandfather clock in the living room sounded through the screened windows.

There was deepening friendship, but there was also something more…an unspoken, growing awareness that she sensed with every encounter.

She bent to snap a few dead blooms from the massive geraniums flanking the back porch steps, then straightened and surveyed her yard. She caught a flicker of movement across the street. "Joel?"

She turned, smiling, but it wasn't Joel. It was someone in the shadows—bulkier, with rounded shoulders. Definitely a man, though she couldn't make out his features.

Emboldened by the arrival of several cars in the vet clinic parking lot next door, she strode to the corner of the café and braced her hands on the top rail of the porch. "Hey!"

The figure shrank back.

"Hey, you! What are you doing over there?"

Several people in the parking lot turned and peered at her over the line of bushes flanking her fence.

Thankful for their presence, she stepped on an upside-down clay pot, vaulted over the fence and hurried up to the front sidewalk.

The man appeared momentarily confused—wavered—then he struck out at a fast pace and disappeared around the corner. A moment later, an engine roared to life and a vehicle sped away.

Shaking, she leaned over and braced her palms on her knees.

It hadn't been someone out for a walk. A prospective buyer sure wouldn't have been spooked when she called out to him.

And if she wasn't mistaken, the guy had matched Anna's description of Hubie Post.

AFTER BUSTLING Sophie and Viper into the café, Beth doubled-checked the padlocks on the yard gates and the doors, then speed dialed both Joel and the sheriff.

Joel had been at the clinic and arrived immediately, followed by Walt a few minutes later. "Are you okay? Is Sophie?"

"He didn't say a word, whoever he was—but he sure acted guilty." She glanced over at Sophie, who was coloring at her table in the corner. "He stared for a while, and he took off like a rocket when I ran out to the road. Nobody would do that if they didn't have something to hide."

"Have you checked everything here?"

"The main floor is untouched, far as I can tell. Nothing is missing from the cash register. I haven't been upstairs, but the door to the stairs was still locked so I'm sure it must all be fine."

"Let me go up there," Joel said. "Walt, would you keep an eye on Sophie?"

"No problem." Walt joined Sophie at her table. "Hey, squirt, can I color, too?"

Beth watched Sophie's face light up, knowing how much the child missed having a father, and wishing she could turn back the clock to when life had seemed so humdrum, so normal and safe. Had she ever really thought her life boring, and wished for something exciting? Had she ever been that foolish?

"Key?" Joel asked.

She jingled through her ring of keys, and unlocked the privacy door to the apartment stairs, but stood aside when Joel insisted on going up alone.

She waited, her tension rising when he didn't call for her to come on up right away. She could hear his heavy steps moving from one room to the next. The creaking of the old floorboards. Once, a soft curse.

"Hey, I think you'd better come up here," he finally called out. "But don't touch anything."

Fear washed through her as she took the stairs one by one, her hand trembling on the handrail.

It didn't take any imagination to guess what she'd find...though when she reached the upper landing, she felt her heart plummet to her feet.

The living room bookshelves were now empty. End table drawers had been jerked out and thrown across the room. A sea of books and papers was strewn on the floor. "My God," she whispered, her voice dull with shock. "My home. Everything. It's *ruined.*"

In the tiny kitchen area, every drawer had been emptied on the floor. In the bedrooms the same had happened to the bureaus and closets. Linens on both beds had been pulled off, and the mattresses were askew.

The stacks of cardboard boxes in the corner of her room had been slashed open and dumped on her bed.

She picked up a pillow that had been ripped open and sank into a wooden rocker in the living area, trying to catch her breath. *"Why?"*

"Obviously, you have something that this guy needs. Badly."

"But I don't!"

"He—or they—sure think so."

"You think it's more than one?"

He toed over an empty cardboard box. "Maybe two. Not more, or it would be too memorable to any passersby, seeing three unfamiliar people around town."

"There are very few passersby out here, though. Most cars pull into the clinic and don't come clear to the dead end. And even farther up Canyon Street, the front yards are deep and the trees and privacy hedges are pretty dense, so few of those houses have a clear view of the street."

"True." Joel leaned down to turn a drawer over. Underneath was a pile of Sophie's little footed pajamas in pinks and yellows and purples.

Beth flinched at the sight of them. "This could be totally unrelated. But if this was the guy from Chicago, he probably figures I have piles of money somewhere. But that's totally ridiculous."

"And imagining that a stranger wouldn't be noticed in a town this size sort of defies logic, too."

"How do you know he hasn't?"

"I've been asking around." Joel moved to a corner of the living room, where there'd been cardboard boxes stacked five high. Now, they'd been ripped open with jagged slashes of a box cutter, leaving a snowdrift of documents on the floor. "What was this?"

"Everything from Patrick's files and desk. Believe me, I went through all of it before moving here, looking for any possible clues." She frowned, then shook her head. "It's mostly just old tax records. Receipts. Warranties."

"All the doors were locked?"

"Certainly." Her voice turned wry as she slowly rose from the chair, feeling as if she'd aged a hundred years. "Guess it didn't help much, even with the new locks."

He started gathering loose papers and tapping them into neat stacks, while Beth began folding the clothes that had been strewn everywhere. "At least you and Sophie weren't here."

From downstairs came the sound of deep male voices, then footsteps up the steps. Dan Talbot appeared at the door, clipboard in hand, his sheriff's badge glinting in a stream of sunlight from one of the high windows.

After surveying the damage, he came out into the living room and shook his head. "After your call, I sent my deputy out to look. Hubie isn't in town, ma'am. Leastways, far as anyone can tell. No one's seen him in days." The sheriff eyed Beth thoughtfully, then pulled out an official-looking mug shot of a man with heavy jowls and a bleak expression. "You sure you saw him?"

She studied the photo. "I didn't see his face, but from his shape and size—he seemed to match Anna's description of Hubie."

"Not likely, but this time I'm dusting for prints."
He lifted the small case. "And if your guy is in the
system, we're going to find out who it is."

# CHAPTER FIFTEEN

BEFORE SHE'D FELT COLD, SHAKEN. In a daze. Now, as she continued to pick up the wreckage in the apartment, she felt only simmering anger at whoever had trashed her apartment.

Walt lingered and entertained Sophie until there was some semblance of order, but then sent her upstairs when he had to leave for emergency surgery. Joel stayed to help.

"This just seems like an act of hatred," she said quietly, so Sophie couldn't hear. "What's the point of slashing pillows—even the mattresses?"

"Your friend might've thought you'd hidden something in them. Or maybe he was getting a little frustrated." Joel finished duct-taping a box shut and looked up at her with a glint in his eye. "I wouldn't mind camping out here for a few nights to see if I could catch this guy in the act, but then you'd either be alone at my place, or in possible danger here. Neither option sounds good."

"At least the deputy is going to cruise around town for a few nights."

"Believe me, they have to cover a whole county, so they can't spend a lot of time on a series of break-ins where there hasn't even been theft. Short-staffed as they are, I don't blame them. This sort of thing gets even less attention in most suburban areas—there's just not enough cops to follow up."

Beth took the box from him and put it on the stack of others containing winter clothes. "At least my security system will be installed by the end of next week. I know how ineffective you think it'll be, but it's something."

She reached for a golf jacket on the floor, her hand trembling as a rush of memories flooded back. "My word."

"What's wrong?" Joel looked over at her with immediate concern.

"I just forgot I kept it, that's all." She stroked the well-worn poplin material. "Almost all of Patrick's clothing went to Goodwill six months after he died. It's such a good cause, and there didn't seem to be a reason to keep everything…" Her eyes burned at the memory of packing his things away. "I just kept a few things. He called this one his 'lucky jacket.' He wore it all the time."

"You should keep it, then." Joel started filling another box with her spare blankets.

She kneeled down and straightened out the jacket's wrinkles against the floor, zipped it, and smoothed her hands over the crumpled fabric.

Coins jingled against each other, so she unzipped it and searched the two inner pockets.

The first held several quarters and a five-dollar bill. The second yielded a folded stack of five or six receipts. "Odd," she mused. "I thought I'd checked all of his pockets already."

She unfolded the papers and spread them out on the floor at her knees. At first the jumble of numbers made no sense. She stared, turned them upside down. Drew in a sharp breath, then sat back. "This can't be. Patrick didn't—I *know* he didn't do this."

They were receipts from the Beaufort Casino.

Beth added them up in her head, feeling a sudden wave of nausea rise in her stomach. How could it be possible?

Joel dropped the box and moved over to her side, picked up first one receipt and then another. He whistled under his breath. "So mild-mannered Patrick wasn't exactly who he seemed."

Her first impulse was to slug his arm for daring to say those words aloud. Her second was to rip the receipts to bits before the truth settled in any deeper.

Joel gently took her hands in his before she could do it. "This might be a lead, Beth."

"A lie," she whispered. "He was living a lie, and I never even guessed. How—"

She closed her eyes, remembering the late-night meetings. The times he'd fumed about being sent on business trips. The odd comment from Patrick's boss at one of the Christmas parties, about her husband's health. Had Pat ever called in sick to cover for going to the track or casinos?

*Lies. All lies.*

Joel rubbed the backs of her hands gently with his thumbs, his voice gentle and low. "Bets this large aren't casual entertainment, honey. This is damned serious."

Her eyes flew open. "If he had someone harassing him to pay up…"

Sophie wandered over, her eyes filled with worry. "I can't find Maisie, Momma. I need my baby."

"I'll help you look, sweetie." Beth scrambled to her feet and began searching. "Did you have her last night, or did you leave her here?"

Sophie's lower lip trembled. "I don't know!" Her voice rose to a wail. "Maybe a bad man took her away."

Beth gathered her into her arms and gave her a long hug, then kissed the top of her head. "I won't let any bad men hurt her, I promise. Should I check downstairs, too?"

At the child's tearful nod against her shoulder, Beth released her. "You wait here, and I'll be right back. Okay?"

Beth dashed down the stairs and took a quick survey of the darkened café and Sophie's play corner, and then went into the kitchen to hunt.

At the soft sound of the bell over the door—

hadn't she locked it after Walt left?—she popped out of the kitchen doors with a smile. "I'm sorry, we're not open until—"

Her heart faltered.

Just inside was a tall, hulking man, his shoulders rounded, his face cast in shadow by the sunlight streaming in behind him.

Hubie Post.

She held her breath, uncertain whether she should scream, race for the phone, or just say hello.

"I watched," he mumbled in a hoarse baritone. "But I can't no more."

She eased forward an inch or two, trying to avoid looking at the phone lying on the lunch counter.

One press of a speed-dial button would call Joel's phone and alert him…but what if he brought Sophie down, too? If this man overpowered Joel…

She hesitated. Took another small step.

Hubie immediately took a wary step back against the screen door.

"Y-you watched? Who?" Her fear faded, and her anger rose, hot and fierce and protective. "My *daughter?*"

"Can't now, or I be in trouble." He shook his shaggy head. "Crystal said to, but I can't."

"*Crystal?* She's…dead." Beth took another small step and Hubie backed out of the door, pushing it open with his shoulder. "Did you tear up my apartment? Were you in here?"

The man lifted his head enough that she could see a wild glint in them. He dropped something, then spun around and was gone.

But just inside the door, he'd left Sophie's bedraggled doll.

BETH EXAMINED THE DOLL carefully before handing it to Sophie, then sent her over to the play corner with a glass of milk and a peanut butter sandwich.

Keeping the child in her line of sight, she lowered her voice. "Hubie said he couldn't 'watch,' because he'd get in trouble. Why would he say that? Seems pretty obvious to me, if he's gotten in trouble before."

"Maybe he wasn't referring to stalking children. Did he know Crystal?"

Beth raised her hands in front of her, palms up. "I have no idea. Maybe he's hallucinating about talking to her."

"Or he promised her something a long time ago." Joel flipped out his cell phone and talked to Walt for a few minutes, then clipped the phone back onto his belt. He shook his head. "Crystal was known for taking in strays and trying to help them back on their feet, but Walt doesn't remember anything about Hubie. Then again, Walt's busy in his clinic and wouldn't have seen everything going on over here. He's also out here just during business hours, barring emergencies."

"Hubie seemed really nervous, and he practically ran from me. It's hard imagining him breaking into my place and ransacking it."

"Except that he managed to get in your front door just now. You want to call the sheriff, or should I?"

She nodded. "I will, definitely. I'd swear that I locked it after Walt left. And now that I think about it, how could Hubie appear out of nowhere? Talbot said he hadn't been around town in a long while."

"If he picked the lock, then maybe he is the one who broke in before."

"Except something just doesn't seem right. He was almost...apologetic. And maybe I'm wrong, but I got the sense that he isn't really someone to fear." She glanced at the clock on the wall. "I've got to get busy. I open in just over an hour."

"Tell me what to do, and I'll pitch in, okay?" Joel reached into a drawer behind the lunch counter and tossed a blue-and-white checkered apron to her, then rummaged around until he found a plain blue one for himself. "No sense having you here alone. Anything else I've got to do can wait."

ON SATURDAY, all of the café's tables were filled. On Monday, maybe half. On Tuesday, the count was down to five patrons including Walt and Loraine, who cast sympathetic glances toward Beth during their meal and made her feel even worse.

At this rate, there'd soon be no one at all.

"First week of summer vacation," Walt said.

"Everyone goes on vacation," Loraine added.

In ranch country? That didn't seem likely.

But Gina, who'd stopped by for a take-out sandwich, nodded in agreement. "People are busy or gone right now, but just wait. The teachers still have another week, but they'll be done next Friday. Then they'll be looking for things to do!"

But when Beth ran into Walt's housekeeper Maria at the grocery store, she found out the truth.

Her eyes downcast, Maria met her in the produce section and sidled close. "I'm sorry about the news," she whispered. "The inspectors are too tough, no?"

"Inspectors?" Beth looked blankly at her. "What inspectors?"

Two vertical lines formed between Maria's eyebrows. "The ones who check the food. There were others who came?"

Mystified, Beth shook her head. "There haven't been any, since before we opened. And then the café was given a top rating for sanitation and the proper equipment."

The disbelief in Maria's eyes was obvious. "I heard it after mass, just yesterday. Two people, food poisoning. Just last week."

"There've been no such cases. *None.* And no one from the state has come out to follow up any complaints, I promise you." Beth thought fast. "All of the restaurant inspections are on the county's Web site—did anyone think to check? Or to call the county health department?"

"No…" Maria's frown cleared. "I heard people talking, and felt bad for you. Word travels fast in small towns."

And would be hard to stop. Unless… "What day does the local paper come out?"

"Wednesday for Lone Wolf. Friday for the one in Horseshoe Falls. The other small towns, I don't know. You want to put in an ad?"

"I was thinking more along the lines of an article, if I can swing it."

A wide smile spread across Maria's face. "Ahhh. There, I can help you. My niece Yolanda writes obituaries for the *Lone Wolf Sentinel*. Maybe she'll write something about your restaurant, too, eh?"

"Perfect. If she'd like to spread her wings a little, maybe she can do some research, and help me figure out where those rumors came from—and why."

YOLANDA PROVED TO BE a stunning little gal with waist-length black hair, flashing black eyes and a flair for the dramatic, who was, like, *totally* thrilled at the opportunity to write about someone who wasn't dead.

She was also a high school junior who wasn't

likely to be doing any serious investigative reporting in the near future.

Still, she wrote a nice, short article on the inaccurate gossip circulating about Crystal's Café, explained how to check inspection reports on the Internet, and even managed to slip in an overawed summary on the café's security system, which had been installed Thursday. She also convinced her father—owner of the paper—to let Beth run a free ad.

On Friday morning Yolanda brought a copy of the paper to the café and presented it to Beth with flourish. "This is the start of my real career," she said dreamily. "Today, Lone Wolf. Tomorrow, the *New York Times*."

Beth hid a smile. "The *Times?*"

"Well, maybe after college," she added with a blush. "We have copies in our school library, and it's awesome."

Beth skimmed her article and gave her a quick hug. *"Perfect."*

Yolanda worried at her lower lip. "You don't think the security thing should've been, like, a surprise? You know, to catch people in the act?"

"Believe me, I'd rather they'd know about it, assume the worst and stay away," Beth said dryly.

"Whatever." The girl's eyes gleamed. "I think it'd be cool to give some dude a real heart attack when he's doing something bad." She looked at her watch and sighed dramatically. "I gotta go home and watch my little brother."

On an impulse, Beth called out to her when she reached the door. "If your article drums up more business, I might be looking for some help with both the café and my daughter. Would you be interested?"

She stopped dead in her tracks and whirled around. "*Would* I! There aren't *any* jobs around here."

"Stop back in a couple days and I'll let you know."

The girl nodded, and walked out with great decorum, but once the door closed behind her, Beth heard a wild whoop of joy.

Beth turned back to Sophie, who was quietly turning the pages of one of her favorite storybooks, and felt a familiar stab of guilt.

Sophie hadn't been to Anna's in over a month now, and had only occasional play dates with Gina's daughter. Having an exuberant teenager play with her for a few hours a day while Beth worked would be a nice, temporary solution, until they were ready for the move to Montana.

"Hey, sweetie, let's read for a while before Momma has to get to work, okay?"

"'Kay." Sophie yawned and snuggled close.

Beth savored the soft, sweet warmth of her little body and began reading.

Halfway through the book, the telephone rang. And rang, and rang. Beth kept reading, but then finally gave up and pulled the portable receiver from her pocket.

The voice was instantly recognizable. Roger

Bennings, the owner of the company where Patrick had worked. Her heart sank. "*Roger.* I...haven't talked to you in a long time."

"I want to know if you've reconsidered," he snapped.

She felt a great weight press down on her chest. "About what?"

"I know you fooled the cops. And I know you think you've gotten away with this, but you won't. You and your husband nearly ruined my company."

"I don't have your money," she said wearily. "I have no idea where it is. Maybe you need to look at someone else."

"You'd like that. But I'm not a fool, and if I don't have the answers I want by the end of this month, I'll be hauling you in to court. You understand?"

"The police investigation—"

"They screwed up, and so did your husband's supervisor, for letting this happen. But I'll be taking things into my own hands from here on out. I've fired Ewen, and if you don't want trouble, you'd better plan on cooperating."

He'd called several times right after Patrick's death. His hollow condolences and subtle, prying questions had made her skin prickle, but he'd never made her feel this uneasy. "Are you threatening me?" she asked coldly. "If you are, I plan to report this to the police."

"It's no threat, Ms. Lindstrom. It's a fact. Go ahead, report it to the police. They're ramping up their investigation, and I'm sure they'd like a chance to talk to you again."

## CHAPTER SIXTEEN

"YOU MUST'VE HAD one hell of a day," Joel said as he forked a rib eye onto Beth's plate.

The aroma of prime, mesquite-grilled beef made her mouth water as she sliced off a stack of small pieces for Sophie and slid them over onto the child's plate. She cut her own baked potato lengthwise and gave Sophie half of that as well, with a generous dollop of butter and sour cream.

"I must look awful."

He automatically passed her the steak sauce. "Not awful, never that. Just tired."

Beth served Sophie a small piece of corn on the cob and garlic-buttered French bread, then passed the serving plates to Joel.

They'd settled into a comfortable routine, each taking care of part of the supper meal. The companionable process had become a highlight of her days, while the long, late nightly talks out on the porch swing had been even better—as long as they veered carefully away from Joel's past.

It would all end tomorrow, when she and Sophie moved back to the café apartment, and just the thought of leaving made her feel…lonely. Which was ridiculous, because that apartment was where they belonged, and this had always been just a temporary situation. She'd known that from the start.

"You don't have to leave," Joel said, his gaze on hers. "You're still better off here. And why move twice, if you plan on leaving Texas in August?"

"We've imposed for over two weeks already."

"It was never an imposition."

"And I really should get back there, so I can start trying to build up the breakfast business. There hasn't been even one prospective buyer so far."

A corner of Joel's mouth lifted. "There's always Tracy."

Beth snorted. "Only as a last resort, and maybe not even then."

His smile widened. "Take a look."

She followed his gaze to Sophie, whose eyelids were drooping. "Sweetie, it's time to eat."

Sophie's head bobbed up, but then she started to slump in her chair. "Excuse me. I think I'd better change her into her jammies and brush her teeth so she can go to sleep. She's had a long day."

Beth took her back to the bedroom and got her ready for bed, then stayed until Sophie was sound asleep. Leaving the bedroom door open, she went back to the kitchen and found Joel waiting, with both of their dinners in the oven turned on low. "You didn't have to wait for me."

"I wanted to." He managed to pull a sad face. "After tonight, I'll be eating alone."

Beth laughed. "From what I've seen of the interested and available young women in this town, you'd never have to worry about that."

"But would they be good company? That's the real question."

"Probably a better bet than a widow with financial troubles, a child and someone from her past lurking about." She kept her tone light. "I'm afraid I'm not a very good bet for anyone."

He frowned. "What happened today?"

"Nothing, really."

"Did Hubie show up again?" He studied her face. "You look stressed."

"No…I just had another call from Patrick's old boss. He says he's still sure I can access all the money that disappeared, and he wants it back or he's taking me to court."

"How can he do that? Does he have any proof?"

"He plans to investigate until he does." She toyed with a slice of her steak. "But I can't tell him any more than I told the police. I don't *know* anything."

"Then you have nothing to worry about."

She exhaled slowly. "Until I found those gambling receipts, I never thought Patrick would do anything wrong. Now I wonder if he could've been frantic over being deep in debt and afraid I'd find out. Maybe he gambled even more, trying to win it all back."

"Which never happens. Though in the meantime, he could've had someone pressuring him for the money."

She closed her eyes against a very real possibility that had been preying on her thoughts all day. "Maybe…he was gambling to try to pay back money he'd 'borrowed' from the company. What if he really *was* depressed, and did try to kill us all in the car wreck?"

Her lower lip trembled at the thought of her sweet little girl, and what could have happened on that awful day.

"Awww, Beth. Come here." Joel pushed away from the table and offered her his hand, pulling her into an embrace. Offering her his strength.

She melted into him, her head tucked beneath his chin and welcomed everything he offered. The steady, comforting beat of his heart. The warmth of his hard-muscled chest and the feeling of childlike security while cradled in his arms.

"Whatever happened, it's over. You and Sophie are here, and you're safe. And that's what matters now, right?"

She nodded, holding back the tears she'd refused to shed over the past year. Determined to stay strong and not let them go now.

Joel pulled back to cup her cheek in the palm of one hand, then lifted her face so he could look down into her eyes.

Something between them changed. The air grew heavier. Charged with the electricity of sudden, rising desire that had been held back for too long. His gaze bore into hers for a long moment, silently questioning. Offering space. And then he lowered his mouth to hers for an exquisitely gentle kiss.

He deepened the kiss, sweeping one hand down to the small of her back and pulling her even closer. His mouth was hot and his hands burned and she reacted almost instantly, wanting him. Needing far, far more than just this kiss.

And just that fast, she knew there'd be no turning back.

Because, though she would never tell him, she knew in this moment that she loved him. Not in the quiet, steadfast way she'd loved Patrick, but with a soul-deep awareness that was nearly overwhelming, making her heart ache for him.

Because no matter what happened here tonight, she'd be leaving soon. Leaving his house, then leaving this town, and there were no other options.

He ended the kiss and looked down at her, his eyes dark and intense and infinitely seductive, and she shivered with the realization that he would be nothing like she'd ever experienced before. Again, he was silently giving her a chance to back away, but she no more could have done that than she could still the rapid beat of her heart.

This wasn't just desire.

She felt an aching sweep of need and desperation, because this might be the only chance she'd ever have with him.

After a lifetime of being good and proper and cautious, a heady feeling of recklessness swept through her. She cradled his face between her hands and pulled him down into a kiss that left her shaking and hungry, and if he hadn't held her in his arms she might have simply slid to the floor.

His gaze, hot and dark, now filled with amusement. "Should I take this as a 'yes'?"

She grinned back at him, an exhilarating sense of joy and anticipation welling up inside her. "Only if you want to live."

SHE'D PLANNED TO MOVE back to the apartment on Sunday. By the following Friday, she'd remade and broken her resolution four times, unable to give up the long, companionable evenings—and now, the long, incomparable nights—at Joel's place.

But today she was making a clean break of it, and it was proving to be the hardest thing she'd ever done. It was time to start listening to her head, instead of her foolish heart.

"This is it," she said, loading the last sack of

Sophie's toys into the back of her Bravada, then lifting in Viper's carrier. She rounded the vehicle and reached in the backseat to check Sophie's car seat, then turned to face Joel. She carefully focused on his shoulder, knowing that her determination would evaporate if she lost herself in his dark, compelling eyes. "I—can't thank you enough."

"I still think you should stay." He pulled her into his arms. "At least here, I know you and Sophie are okay."

She leaned into him, savoring his warmth. Resisting the desire to move back in and never leave. "We'll be fine. There's been no trouble for weeks now, so the newspaper article about the security system probably warned people away."

"I wouldn't be so sure."

"And someone trashed my place so thoroughly, it must've been pretty clear that I have nothing worth stealing, and certainly nothing related to the problems at Pat's company. I should be home free."

He pulled back and rested his hands on her shoulders. "If you want me to, I can stay with you a couple nights." A corner of his mouth lifted. "I could toss a sleeping bag into some corner downstairs, for propriety's sake."

She shifted her gaze to his top button, but found herself wanting to nibble it open. Then the ones below it, too. *Bad idea.* "It's Sophie. Here, there's privacy, but there, it would just be too—"

He touched a finger to her lips, then cupped his hands behind her head to draw her into a gentle kiss. "I know."

"And you've got chores here. Your cows, and horses, and Earl…"

"I know. But if you have any trouble— anything at all—promise you'll call me." He brushed a kiss against her forehead then stepped back, setting her free.

Freedom that suddenly made her feel empty. Bereft.

His work was done at both the café and the clinic, and on Wednesday he'd started a job in Prophetsville, thirty miles to the north, so she'd no longer be seeing him at odd times of the day for those casual visits. At the sound of the bells chiming over the front door of the café, her heart wouldn't be making that funny little leap of anticipation.

He might still stop by in the evenings, but it wouldn't ever be the same.

And staying here any longer would just make it all the more painful, because with every day, she fell a little more in love…and she was only fooling herself if she thought there'd ever be a future with him. He'd made that perfectly clear.

Though it didn't matter anyway, because soon she'd need to leave Lone Wolf behind.

Last night she'd taken a hard look at the income she could clear at the café. The heavy burden of taxes on the self-employed. The lack of good benefits that would make it harder to raise Sophie alone.

There was no way she could afford to stay.

COMMITMENT WAS a frightening thing. Since the end of his marriage, just the thought of it made Joel's blood run cold, dredging up the memories of his little girl's death and the bitterness of his divorce. No one had come close to weakening his shell of bone-deep self-preservation.

Until Beth.

And he'd even managed pretty well in that regard, until…hell. Probably five minutes after he met her, though he'd managed to hide his feelings pretty damn well from everyone, including himself. Except perhaps Walt, who'd been giving him knowing looks and helpful advice for the past two months.

Unrequested advice. Every day.

Joel had smiled and politely ignored him. Tried to instantly forget everything the irascible old man said. But now Walt's words haunted him in an endless litany at night.

Words about lost years. Lost chances. Empty lives and foolish men who paid the price for being too dang stubborn for their own good.

The first night after Beth left, Joel resolved to keep some distance, knowing that it was what she wanted, too. By the second night he was slamming silverware in the dishwasher and even snapped at poor old Earl, who'd lumbered into an end table and knocked over a lamp while endlessly searching for his little friend.

Obviously working Joel's guilt to his advantage, the old dog climbed onto his bed during the night… snoring and whuffling, and edging ever closer until he had the dead center of the bed.

But when he draped his long, heavy nose over Joel's ear, that was the final straw.

Joel rose up on one elbow and looked him in the eye. "You, Earl, have got to go."

Earl whined softly, then closed his eyes.

"Now."

The dog didn't even twitch. For an animal that had been totally dominated by a nine-pound ball of fur, he now appeared remarkably unconcerned by his master's voice.

Joel pushed him—at least sixty pounds of dead-weight—to the other side of the bed.

Earl crept back, looking as sorrowful as Joel felt. "Maybe we can get them back," Joel said.

Earl opened his eyes.

"This place was perfect before. And now it's… empty."

His own foolish words came back to him. What he'd said to Beth about his determination to avoid marriage forever, and how he knew he'd never want to be a father again. "And I am just so damned stupid."

At that, the dog lifted his head, and the deep

wisdom in his rheumy old eyes suggested that Earl fully agreed.

Joel thought about what it would take to keep Beth in Lone Wolf and who could help make it happen. How hard could it be?

Surely it couldn't be too late to get this right.

"HIRING YOU WAS the best move I've made," Beth said. She watched Yolanda painstakingly wipe down and sanitize the last table in the café, then carefully put back the condiments and vase of fresh flowers. "Do you have any questions?"

The girl beamed at her. "So I did okay on my first day?"

"Perfect. And thanks to you and the newspaper, business picked up enough to make it possible. This was our best Monday yet."

"You want me to dust?" Yolanda planted her hands on her slim hips and peered up at the decorative coffee tins lined up on top of the china hutch in the corner. "I don't mind."

"I can do that later. I'd rather you took Sophie outside to play for a while. She'd love to swing and play with Viper."

"Viper." Yolanda shuddered. "That's a baaaad name. How about Sweetie Pie. Or Puffy…or Fluff?"

"Have you *seen* her in action?" Beth gave the lunch counter one last swipe with sanitizer solution. "Piranha might work."

Beth watched Sophie happily take Yolanda's hand and go out the back door, then she grabbed the stack of mail on the counter and started flipping through it. With a groan she set it aside. The stack fanned out across the counter.

It had been hard, moving from Joel's place to town.

She'd gone through all the motions at the café, but she hadn't been able to get Joel out of her thoughts. Should she have stayed? Enjoyed as much of him as she could, until the time when she needed to pack for Montana?

The painful wrench of her heart confirmed her decision. It had been wise to make a clean break, so she could heal and move on.

Heaving a sigh, she gathered up the mail to take with her upstairs, but a Montana postmark on a thick envelope caught her eye. She slid a fingernail under the flap and pulled out a two-page letter, some clippings from a newspaper and a dozen photographs.

Her entire future, delivered for a dollar's worth of stamps.

She sat on a swivel stool at the counter and glanced at the article about a new steak house opening on the west side of Billings, then painstakingly tried to decode her sister's looping scrawl.

Melanie had found a nice little two-bedroom rambler just a few blocks from her home, priced below market as the owners had already moved to

Arizona. Low down payment. New roof. Fenced yard. The photos showed it from all angles, inside and out. It looked...nice. Well kept.

And boring.

Beth returned to the letter and read more details about the house and about the steak house, which apparently belonged to some childhood friends of Melanie's and needed a manager. The owners had already expressed strong interest in Beth, so if she could just send a résumé...

Melanie, bless her heart, had always been the flighty sister. The one who needed to be advised or bailed out of one situation after another. Yet here, she'd managed to line up a good job and a great deal on a snug little house, and her letter bubbled over with excitement over her finds and the fact that Beth would soon live close by.

She put the letter down and sat back, suddenly tired.

The front doorbell jingled. She looked over her shoulder, ready to let a patron know that the noon serving time was over. Her heart skipped a beat. *"Joel?"*

He'd seemed remote when they'd said their goodbyes at his place on Saturday. She hadn't heard from him since, and that had only confirmed what he'd once said about avoiding commitments. He might as well have said "good riddance" when she drove away.

But now, he emanated a level of energy and anticipation that surprised her. "You look…happy."

He strode across the floor and pulled her into a long, deep kiss that made her toes tingle. "I've been busy. Doing things I should've done a long time ago. And it's all due to Earl."

"Your *dog?*"

He grinned. "Earl made me see the error of my ways. And Walt, of course," he added. "But mostly Earl, because he mopes so well."

"I think that's a standard job description for a bloodhound. Not to take anything away from his skills, or anything."

"Well, I—" Joel's gaze fell to the scattering of photographs and clippings on the counter. He pulled in a slow breath. "What's this?"

"My new life."

From the moment he kissed her, she knew he wanted to ask her to move back to his place. To go back to playing house, having wild and wonderful sex. But though the thought had already started doing dizzy things to her insides, it could have no place in her life. He wanted no commitments. She had responsibilities. A life to build for Sophie. She needed a better career, with good insurance and investment benefits—and that couldn't happen, running a tiny café. But thanks to Melanie, she now had a second chance she could not pass up.

"It's Montana," she added. "A house, a job. Everything."

"But what about…" He floundered. "The café?"

"The Realtor called this morning. She wants to bring over a 'live one'—someone who grew up here and wants to move back." Beth shrugged. "Could be a sale, or maybe not. But business has picked up, and it's only a matter of time."

His expression cooled. "Good news."

"Yes, it is. I guess everything is falling into place." She looked over at the calendar on the wall. "I might even be able to leave a month earlier than I'd planned."

JOEL NODDED TO MARIA, then made his way through Walt's house to the back porch. He smiled when he found his uncle reading a veterinary journal with a highlighter in hand.

Even at seventy-two—long past retirement age— the man loved his profession too much to quit, and still studied like a college student to keep up with current research. As a boy, Joel had admired him. As an adult, he admired Walt even more, for his ethics, wisdom and his meticulous professionalism.

So why had Joel waited so long to take his uncle's words to heart?

"I made flight arrangements this morning." Joel settled into a wicker chair next to Walt's. "Thought you should know that I'll be leaving."

Frowning, Walt lowered the journal and took off his reading glasses. "Leaving?"

"You were right, you know. About everything. Guess I was just too stubborn to see it."

Walt leaned back in his chair and steepled his fingertips. He studied Joel intently, with a hint of a twinkle in his eyes. "This would be about the little lady from Chicago?"

"I didn't think I could ever face the risk of any sort of commitment again. And the thought of another child…" Joel swallowed hard.

"Sophie and her momma are pretty special," Walt said gently.

"If I could be a part of their lives forever, I'd be the luckiest guy on earth. But no matter what Beth's answer is, I need to make sure they'll be safe."

"How can you do that?"

"I've got to go to Detroit for a meeting with my boss, because he still wants me to come back to work. But then I'm going to see some investigators with the Chicago Police Department. Beth's husband got himself in a lot of trouble before he died, and someone is still harassing her over that deal. I'm damn sure going to find out who it is."

# CHAPTER SEVENTEEN

"I'M GOING TO MISS WORKING HERE." Beth leaned against the door to Walt's office, surprised at how sad she felt about it. He'd been like a grandpa to Sophie over the past three months. "The deal did go through."

"It did?" He raised a snowy eyebrow and leaned back in his desk chair. "Now, how do you feel about that?"

"Surprised. A little relieved, because it had to happen." She bit her lip. "And sad. The buyer wanted to close immediately, so I've already started packing."

"So soon? Maybe you shouldn't jump the gun. A gal like you could find another job around these parts and stay." His eyebrow wiggled. "I could take you on full-time."

"I've…already accepted a job in Billings, so that's a done deal. And I've made an offer on a little house, in a school district that has good services for kids who need them. We'll stay with my sister until we have a place of our own."

He pursed his lips. "Seems to me, that little gal's hearing is coming right along."

"She's getting better, just like the doctor thought. But still..." Beth wished it was easier, letting go of a town she'd come to love, and people she cared for. "It's a big school system, and their programs will help her catch up. And as a single mom, I need a good benefits package and a steady salary, so it's all for the best."

"But what about you—is this good for you?" He always seemed to see right through her, to the feelings she tried to hide. And even now she could hear the hint of criticism in his voice. "Leaving us all behind?"

"That's the hardest part." She'd made friends here. She'd fallen in love. And with over seventeen hundred miles between Lone Wolf and Billings, she'd probably never see any of these people again.

"Can't beat a small town," he mused.

"Oh, Walt." She smiled through her sudden tears as she crossed the room to give him a hug. He met her halfway and hugged her right back. "I know that's true."

He waved her into one of the leather upholstered chairs in front of his desk and dropped into the other one. "Have you heard from Joel?"

"Not since last Monday." Seven days and three hours ago, to be precise. Not that she'd paid any attention. "I suppose he's busy with that project in Prophetsville."

"Actually, he finished it, and he's on his way to Detroit."

Startled, she stared at Walt's sad expression. "He's *moving?*"

"Not yet. The department wants him back pretty bad, though. They flew him back there for a meeting. I think they want to offer him a raise and a promotion."

She sank back in her chair, and it took a moment before she could find her voice. "He said he'd never consider it…unless something 'monumental' happened."

"Surprised me, too." Walt looked down at his weathered hands. "But maybe he never found what he was looking for, here."

"What was that?" She held her breath.

"Happiness. A good life…even if he never knew what that should be."

"When did he leave?"

"Flew out last night." Walt's voice sounded weary. "He'll be back in a few days, of course, and then he'll have to decide what to do."

She'd known their relationship was over. She'd been trying to temper her aching sense of loss with the fact that moving to Billings was the right thing to do, because she'd never have a future with a man who wanted to avoid commitment.

But she hadn't expected that he'd leave town without saying farewell, knowing she'd likely be gone by the time he returned. His action told her exactly how little he cared.

"I...suppose I'd better get back home. I'll try his cell phone tonight, just to wish him well."

"Are you okay, sugar?" Walt's voice was laced with concern. "Do you need some water, or something? You look pale."

She gave him another quick hug and managed a wobbly smile. "I'm fine. I just have a lot of packing to do myself."

ON WEDNESDAY, Beth closed the doors of Crystal's Café for the last time. All of her customers showed up early—filling the tables and lunch counter, even signing a waiting list. Her favorites came at the end of her shift.

Walt and Loraine, looking cozier than ever.

Gina, followed by a dozen of her ranch relatives. The two shy, youngest cowboys blushing as they walked in; the older ones clapping Beth on the shoulder and announcing that they were going to miss those fancy pastries she made, and all those "New York" sandwiches that, by golly, tasted pretty damn good.

By the time they all left, Beth was exhausted. A good thing, though, because if there'd been time to think, she might have started to cry. Since talking to Walt, she'd tried calling Joel four times—and had left messages twice.

He hadn't returned her calls.

"You okay, Miz Lindstrom?" Yolanda eyed her over a rack of cups ready to run through the dishwasher. "You aren't like, gonna break down, are you?"

"No. Of course not." Beth managed a watery laugh. "We had a good day, didn't we?"

"I got a whole eight dollars in tips! I sure wish you weren't closing."

"Me, too. But maybe you can get a job with the new owners."

"Will you tell them about me?"

"I've never even met them. It was all handled by their lawyer." Beth had strong suspicions about Tracy and her husband, though the Realtor refused to divulge the names. "I'll write you a glowing reference, though, and they can call me anytime."

After they'd thoroughly cleaned the kitchen, Beth checked on Sophie, who was curled up asleep in her beanbag chair in the play corner, then she pulled two Cokes from the refrigerator and handed one to Yolanda. "Here's a toast—to happy futures."

Yolanda laughed and tapped her can against Beth's, then took a long swallow. She gestured toward the hanging racks of pans and utensils. "The new owner really wants all this stuff?"

Beth shrugged. "They paid for the contents. And where I'm going, I won't be running my own café."

"You don't look happy. I'd be way excited, if I was moving far away."

"It's all just a lot of work. Tonight I've got to finish loading up the rental trailer, and tomorrow I need to be on the road by six."

Yolanda brightened. "Do you need help? I've got three brothers, and they're all football players. They're super strong."

"Believe me, that's the best news I've heard all day."

YOLANDA AND HER BROTHERS proved to be better help than Beth could've hoped for.

By eight o'clock, the only things left in the apartment were two sleeping bags, a small suitcase and Darwin's cat box. Darwin had retreated to the top of the refrigerator in his usual pose, with a foreleg, rear leg and his tail dangling down the front surface like mutant ivy, while Viper had promptly curled up on Beth's sleeping bag—apparently thinking she wouldn't have to share if she got there first.

Once Sophie fell asleep for the night, Beth wandered through the apartment listening to the hollow echo of her footsteps, feeling oddly out of place. "C'mon, Viper, let's get you outside one more time."

The dog dutifully got up, followed her downstairs and into the backyard, where deepening twilight had turned the landscape to shades of indigo. Viper disappeared into the shadows, while Beth sat on the edge of the porch waiting for her to do her business and come back.

The cool evening air was heavy with the scents of late spring wildflowers and the cedars growing along the stream just past the vet clinic. Now and then, the breeze picked up the peppery scent of sagebrush from the vast pasturelands that spread clear to the western horizon.

The mesquite leaves rustled. A cicada buzzed. From somewhere far on the other side of town came the sound of a dog barking.

Leaning back on her elbows, Beth breathed in the scents and lost herself in her memories of the past months, feeling melancholy and alone.

She'd been naïve, imagining that Joel had ever really cared for her. She'd been a convenience, a casual fling that was nothing more than the result of proximity and the long, dark and sultry Texas nights. So far out in the country that the lights of other ranches weren't visible, and stars blanketed the sky, it had seemed as if they were the last people left in the universe.

Viper's low growl brought her sharply to attention. She sat bolt upright and scanned the yard. "Viper?" she called out softly. "Come, girl."

The dog growled louder.

Fear crawled down Beth's spine as she eased back toward the door, ready to turn and run.

Now in the shadows of the porch and out of bright, silvery moonlight, her eyes adjusted. Focused. A towering shape seemed to coalesce from the darkness just beyond the fence.

"H-Hubie?" she whispered.

Viper bolted up the porch steps and leaned against Beth's ankles, her tense body vibrating as she growled.

The figure stepped into a pool of light under the solitary streetlamp at this end of the road. He was a large man, his shaggy head held at an angle, but he was clearly looking in her direction. If it wasn't Hubie, it had to be his twin.

She backed up another foot, and felt for the doorknob behind her back. Eased it open…slowly.

In one swift motion she swept the dog into her arms and whirled around, let herself inside, and shot the dead-bolt lock home.

SHE SPENT THE NIGHT with her hand on her cell phone and Viper at her side, listening to the creaks and groans of the old house as it settled its old bones for the night.

Each noise made her heart stutter and her hand clench around the phone. During the predawn hours, as she watched the unbearably slow march of minutes on the digital clock, she came to realize two things—hardwood floors and sleeping bags were a match made in hell, and that leaving Lone Wolf would be a blessed relief.

Billings was a large city, with a police department. It would offer far faster response times. That snug little house was flanked on all sides with neatly kept photocopies of itself—offering the close proximity and curious eyes of neighbors, who would surely be a deterrent to strangers.

Lone Wolf, Texas, would always have a big part of her heart, but in Billings, she and Sophie would be safe. The sooner they got there, the better.

SOPHIE TUGGED at the hem of Beth's T-shirt. "Momma, can't we go to Olivia's house again?"

Beth reached down to give her a hug, then helped her into the backseat of the SUV. "Remember? We need an early start if we're to make it to our motel tonight."

From the rear of the vehicle came the sounds of Viper clawing at her carrier, and the loud, feral growl of Darwin, who was not pleased with his accommodations, either.

It was going to be a long, long day.

"Can't Darwin sit on my lap?" Sophie kicked her feet against the back of the front seat. Her voice rose to a whine. "I want Darwin with *me!*"

"He's got his food, water and a small litter pan, honey. And he's safer if he isn't running around in the car. What if he jumped out when we stopped at a gas station?"

Sophie's lower lip pushed forward in a pout. "I'd hold him."

"But with those rear claws for traction, he could make his escape all too quickly." Beth dropped a kiss on Sophie's forehead, checked the car seat, then rounded the back of the rental trailer to check the padlock on the back doors.

By the time she turned the key in the ignition, the first rosy blush of dawn was just peeking through the mesquite trees. The vet clinic was still dark, though; the street in front of her house was deserted and the entire town still folded in the soft, misty silence of early morning.

She'd wanted to leave early, before friends and acquaintances began stirring, and then started coming to say their goodbyes all over again.

Already the farewells filled her with a sense of loss, especially the one Joel hadn't even thought to share—an all too painful reminder about just how foolish she'd been, letting herself fall for someone like him.

Reaching across the seat, she pulled a Texas map and a MapQuest route printout from her purse and tossed them on the dashboard. "We're off, honey! A new adventure."

"Maisie!" Sophie's voice rose to a piercing

shriek. She scrambled in her seat, trying to release the safety latch. "I forgot my dolly!"

Beth dropped her forehead briefly to the top of the steering wheel. "Don't worry—I'll get her. Just tell me where she is."

"Back there!"

"Where?" Beth followed Sophie's frantically waving hand to somewhere in the backyard. "The swings?"

At the child's emphatic nod, Beth hopped out of the SUV and jogged over to the swing set, where she found the doll lying on one of the seats.

Sophie gave her a watery smile when she handed over the doll. Sophie hugged the doll fiercely, her tears starting anew. "I don't *wanna* go."

"I know, sweetheart. But your aunt Melanie is waiting for us, and we need to get moving." As she climbed behind the wheel once more, a small, fluttering scrap of paper wedged against the windshield wiper caught her eye.

She grabbed it, tossed it on the seat, then started the vehicle and turned out onto the street before Sophie could think of another excuse to stop.

She drove slowly into town and turned north on Main. In her rearview mirror she glimpsed Walt's vet truck turning west on Saguaro, and another wave of regret tugged at her heart. It was all for the best…so why did she have the feeling that she was making a terrible mistake?

THE CLUSTER OF ACREAGES around town soon gave way to vast, rolling pastureland that spread out to the horizons.

"Are we going back to the other house? With the big dog?" Sophie sat up straighter in her seat and peered out the windows. "I want to see Earl again!"

Beth flicked a glance toward the backseat and shook her head. "He lives on a different highway, honey. Want your coloring book and crayons?"

Sophie flopped back in her seat, pouting. "I need to go potty."

Beth bit back a groan. There wasn't a town for another thirty miles or more, and some of the towns on the map were barely more than a wide spot in the road with a couple of houses and a long-closed tavern.

And Sophie was still *very* particular about the sort of facilities—or lack thereof—that she would use.

"I could just pull over," Beth suggested, glancing over her shoulder with a bright smile. "That would be fast. There's no one around to see."

It was true. There hadn't been a mailbox in miles, and they hadn't met an oncoming car since leaving Lone Wolf. The road was empty save for them and a single car far behind them on the highway.

"I can't." Sophie wiggled anxiously in her seat. "I need a *real* potty. Like at home."

"There are only two choices. Stop by the side of

the road, or hold it until we find a gas station, and that could be another twenty minutes or more." When Sophie didn't answer, Beth slowed down and started watching for a turnoff.

They were truly out in the middle of nowhere now. The hills were higher, with sharp outcroppings of rock jutting from the sparse grass, and sagebrush dotted the landscape. Here and there, deep, rocky ravines slashed the terrain.

The car behind them drew closer. But instead of rocketing past, it slowed.

Beth eased up on the accelerator, encouraging the driver to go around. Instead, the car crept closer.

*Closer.*

She glanced in the side mirrors again, and her heart crawled up into her throat. The driver's face was shaded with a ball cap and dark sunglasses.

And now he was practically on her bumper, the threat unmistakable…and there hadn't been a ranch sign for miles.

He edged even closer.

She felt the unmistakable jolt of his car ramming hers.

She stepped on the gas, but he stayed right with her, and hit her bumper again. The SUV fishtailed wildly across both lanes before she could get it back under control and shove down the accelerator.

The car fell behind—then loomed larger and larger in the side mirrors.

"Momma! What's wrong?" Sophie cried out. "I'm scared!"

Beth steadied the car. Fumbled for her cell phone. Flipping it open, she held her breath for a second, almost afraid to look for reception bars on the screen.

Just *one*. And with these deep, rock-strewn hills, that one could fade at any moment.

Trying to slow her racing heart, she hit the 911 speed dial button. Through static, she could barely hear the dispatcher's voice. She quickly gave her location, praying the woman could make out her words—then she punched Joel's number, and prayed even harder.

He'd been a cop. He'd know how to help her, if he was back from Detroit and could make it out here in time. *Please Lord, let him pick up this call.*

## CHAPTER EIGHTEEN

THE VEHICLE BEHIND HER fell back when a sporty little car roared toward them from over the hill ahead. Her hands shaking, she tried flashing her headlights but it flew past in a crimson blur, its driver oblivious to her panic.

Again she hit the speed dial on her phone. Spared a glance at the trip odometer.

And lost the connection when the road dipped.

At the top of the next rise she tried again. No answer. But this time she managed to leave a frantic message.

The car behind her drew steadily closer.

She accelerated. Seventy-five. Eighty.

How far could the next town be? Or some sign of inhabitants—a place where she could turn off that would lead her to people who might provide safety?

Just over the next hill a ranch sign flew past— with too little advance warning to make a turn. Ahead, she could see the road snake through some river-bottom land and thick stands of cypress and cedar, then it rose into even rougher terrain.

In the backseat, Sophie had started to whimper, and now she was crying, her voice laced with terror. "Stop, Momma—please, stop!"

Beth fought to stay calm. "Soon, sweetheart."

But like a powerful animal overtaking its prey, the car behind them pulled closer. Veered into the oncoming lane. And then began to edge past the Bravada.

She couldn't outrun it. If it ran them off the road now, they'd be airborne on a trip to certain death.

She let up on the accelerator. Gripped the steering wheel. And began feathering the brakes. Then she hit them harder and felt the vibration of the antilock brakes fighting for purchase on the smooth asphalt. The other car held even with them for a split second, then it shot past, its taillights glowing red and brakes squealing. It swerved wildly, directly in their path. *Oh, God...oh, God...*

*"Momma! It's him,"* Sophie screamed. *"It's him!"*

A split second later the Bravada smashed the back end of the car and shot over the shoulder of the highway. Weightless, it hung in the air for one breathless, endless moment, when time stood still.

Then the SUV hit the ground with bone-jarring force and rocketed down a rocky, twisted path, careening past boulders and scrub cedars. Ricocheting against the high walls of the ravine.

Near the bottom it arced up a steep incline and paused. Then tumbled sideways in a cloud of dust, rolling twice amidst the nightmarish sounds of popping glass and screeching metal.

And then, silence. Total, eerie silence.

Dazed, Beth stared blankly at the sagebrush plastered against the windshield, then realized the Bravada was upside down and her head was pounding.

Pawing at the deflated air bag, choking on the roiling dust, she tried to clear her scrambled thoughts filled with nightmarish images of their downward plunge.

Flashes of Patrick, screaming as he gripped the wheel.

*Sophie shrieking—or was it me?*

Sagebrush and sand and scrub cedars, the vision intertwined with a looming bridge abutment. Massive. Gray. Spattered with blood.

*OhmyGod...OhmyGod...*

Nausea welled up in her throat. But she was caught—suspended in her seat belt, her head against the buckled roof. And Sophie... OhmyGod...

"Sophie? *Sophie!*"

Eerie, deathlike silence.

Panic shot through her as she struggled to release her seat belt. The side window was gone. She crawled through it to the sharp stones outside, barely aware of the warm, sticky flow of blood running down the side of her face.

Somewhere along the way, the trailer had broken free and was nowhere in sight. The SUV's rear door was open, twisted at a crazy angle. She crawled in to reach the car seat, her heart racing. "Sophie!"

"M-momma?" Sophie's eyes were wide and dazed in her pale face.

Relief rushed through Beth like a tidal wave. "Oh, sweetheart. Are you okay? Do you hurt anywhere?"

Sophie's stunned expression turned to awareness, then terror, her eyes welling with tears. *"S-scared."*

"I know you are. I'm getting you out of here. Just hold on."

Sophie started to whimper. "Are we gonna die, like Daddy?"

"Of course not," Beth soothed. "I just need to…"

She struggled against gravity and Sophie's weight, trying to release the shoulder straps, her fingers slippery with her own blood. There…almost…

Then Sophie tumbled out onto Beth's chest, nearly taking her breath away.

"Okay, now we're going to just ease out of here. I'm in the way, so I need to back out first. All right?"

"You're bleeding!"

"It's just a tiny cut on my head, but those always bleed a lot. No worries." Sophie came out after her, scrambling frantically to be free of the car. As soon as Beth got to her feet, Sophie launched into her arms and hugged her around the neck. "I was so scared, Momma."

"I know. Me, too." Beth ran a hand over the child's arms and legs, then set her gently back on the ground to get a good look. No blood. Not even a scratch. "I can't believe it. But now—"

From far up the ravine came the sound of rocks clattering down the rocky bank. *Footsteps?*

On its wild, tortuous path down through the ravine, the Bravada had torn through heavy sagebrush and scraggly young cedars, and had come to rest behind some heavy undergrowth. It was out of sight from the road, but it wouldn't take long for their pursuer to find it—and them—if they didn't start moving, fast.

Beth took Sophie's hand and started through the underbrush, then turned back and grabbed her purse out of the Bravada. But the cell phone—she dug frantically through the jumble of clothes and books and toys that had been tossed during the crash. Oh, God—where was the phone?

From the back of the SUV, Darwin grumbled from the depths of his cage and Viper whined, pawing anxiously to get out. But she'd have to come back—there was no way she could lug them, and if Viper ran loose, she might all too easily alert their pursuer to the direction they'd gone.

"There it is, Momma!" Sophie ran forward and grabbed the phone from the ground by the rear bumper. "And my Maisie, too!"

"Super, honey." Beth pocketed the phone, fixing a smile on her face. She hurried to the other side of the vehicle and wrenched open the glove box to retrieve an old can of pepper spray. She fumbled with it. Dropped it twice before she could steady her shaking hands and stash it in her purse. "Now listen. We have to be quiet. Understand? I don't think that man is very nice, and we don't want him following us, okay?"

Her doll clutched tightly to her chest, Sophie nodded, her eyes somber and her lower lip trembling. "He killed my daddy."

"No, sweetie. It was a car accident."

"He was *there*. He made it happen."

Beth blinked and struggled to arrange the fractured images that were spinning through her brain. There *had* been another car the night Patrick was killed. Hadn't there?

But none of it made sense, and she didn't have time to sort it out. "We've got to hurry. Let's go." Beth took her hand and started off into the brush, trying to stay on the rocks instead of the sandy soil and heading parallel to the highway.

Sophie cried out as she slipped on the loose gravel and nearly fell.

Beth picked her up and brushed a kiss against her tearstained cheek, but kept moving. Moving. Forcing her way through thick, pungent sagebrush. Dodging wicked bushes with long thorns whose name she couldn't recall.

The sun broke free of the clouds overhead, washing out the arid landscape in harsh, bright light. Sweat trickled down her back as she struggled to keep going. Then she stopped, held a finger to her lips and listened.

She could hear him crashing through the brush. Silence…then the squeal of metal. A thudding sound. Glass breaking. He was searching the *car?*

Black spots danced in front of her eyes as a wave of dizziness washed through her. She reached up and felt her hair, sticky and matted.

What if she passed out? Only a fool would leave witnesses, and if he thought either of them had seen his face…then Sophie…

Gritting her teeth she straightened and shifted Sophie's weight to her back. "Hold tight—around my neck," she whispered, capturing the child's legs in the crook of her elbows.

She forced herself to jog at a steady pace, dodging between stands of scrub cedars for cover, weaving through sagebrush and some sort of low-lying cactus. Sweat dripped down her face and between her breasts.

"Momma, I still gotta go potty," Sophie whispered brokenly against Beth's ear.

A thicker stand of cedar lay ahead, maybe the distance of a city block. And if she angled up the rocky slope to the right, the highway should be up there somewhere.

Or…was it? How far had they gone down into the ravine—and had their direction changed? And what if she'd started out on foot in the wrong direction? Even a few degrees could mean the difference in finding that endless ribbon of asphalt and the possibility of a passing rancher.

Or miles of vast, deserted Texas landscape.

"Just up there, Sophie…" Heat rose in shimmering waves from the hard, sandy earth, making it difficult to breathe. Sophie grew heavier with each step. "And…then…we'll stop for a second."

She struggled on, nearly collapsing when they reached the cover of the trees, but for once, Sophie didn't argue about the lack of facilities.

As soon as she was finished, Beth moved deeper into the trees. "Quiet," she whispered. She put two fingers to her lips. "Stay right here and *don't move.*"

"Momma!" Sophie launched into her arms, wrapping herself around Beth's waist. "Don't go!"

"It's okay, I'm just going to look behind us." Beth gently extricated herself from Sophie's grasp and checked her cell phone. No reception. "Now, don't make a sound, okay? And stay still. Let's see how well you can play 'statue.'"

Beth wound back through the tangle of cedar branches and studied the terrain. The rocky slope was empty. Silent.

And then she heard a man's distant, harsh curse…the voice oddly familiar.

He rounded a rocky outcropping, his eyes on the ground, a ball cap and sunglasses obscuring his face. He was traveling faster than she could ever travel with Sophie.

She sank back behind the branches, her heart racing. He looked up and seemed to stare straight at her. Then stopped and looked down the hill, as if debating which way she'd gone.

Beth whirled around and hurried to Sophie. "We have to go—now. Don't make a single sound. Okay?"

Taking her hand, she hurried through the trees…and stopped in her tracks.

There'd been cover behind them. Boulders and scrub vegetation. A twisting path up out of the ravine. Ahead lay a gentle, grassy slope and beyond that, what appeared to be miles of open pastureland marked only with a scattering of low sagebrush and an occasional cedar. There was no place to hide.

To the right, a rugged, rocky wall rose steeply above them. Even if they could make it, it would take more time than they had—but there was no other choice.

Beth kneeled down and took Sophie's shoulders. "We've got to go up those rocks. It's going to be hard, honey. But you have to be very, very quiet—even if you get an owie."

Sophie appeared numb and frightened, but she nodded.

"And you keep going, no matter what. There's probably a road up there. If the sheriff or Joel got my message, they might drive by sometime soon. If you see their cars, it's okay—you can wave them down. Understand?"

A tear fell down Sophie's dusty face. "But what about you?"

If she had to, she'd veer off in a different direction to draw the man's attention away from Sophie, but that was a plan better left unsaid. "I'll be coming right along, so don't worry—if I fall behind, just keep going."

Beth picked up Sophie and ran to the right, picking her way through fallen boulders. Boosting Sophie ahead of her when the terrain rose steeply. The sharp rocks tore at her jeans and her palms as she climbed, lifting Sophie to the next shelf when the rise was too steep.

The sun blazed overhead, hot and relentless. Sweat trickled down Beth's back and face, stinging her abrasions. Sophie cried out and turned partway, showing Beth her bloodied palm. "It'll be okay, sweetheart, we're halfway there."

But still, they were exposed to the view from below. And at any minute…

What if the guy was *armed?*

The next ledge was about as long as a sofa. Sophie sank down on it. "I'm too *tired,* Momma."

"But we've got…"

At the sound of a branch breaking, she glanced down. They'd made it a couple hundred feet…but now, the man was just stepping beyond the cedars. Fear shot down Beth's spine. If he happened to look up…

"Back! Get back!" Beth said. Sophie shrank against the wall of rock behind her and Beth did, too.

Were they out of sight?

At her feet lay a good-sized rock—maybe the size of a softball. Beth leaned forward and hefted its weight. Peered over the edge of the shelf.

He was still standing there, clearly trying to catch his breath, bent over with his hands on his thighs. But any minute…

She eased into a crouch. Lifted the rock, then sent it arcing out into the cedars with every ounce of her strength.

The man didn't turn around. More desperate now, she grabbed another rock and sent it flying, as far as she could back into the trees.

This time, he straightened abruptly, spun around and stared, then hurried back the way he'd come.

"Now, honey—let's move—fast! He thinks we're still down there."

Sophie scrambled up ahead of her, with Beth's hand at her waist. Just fifty feet from the top. Forty. Thirty—

"Momma!" Sophie screamed. She awkwardly turned and fell, her weight knocking Beth off her feet. They slid on the loose rock, the rough edges tearing at Beth's T-shirt and biting into her back. Pain ripped through her and it was all she could do to hold back a sudden cry.

A volley of rocks tumbled down the cliff face, bouncing and clattering, the noise loud as cannon shot as it echoed across the land below.

Beth closed her eyes and said a swift, silent prayer. Sophie hovered over her, her eyes huge. She pointed uphill. "*Snake,* Momma. *Big.*"

Beth gingerly rolled to her knees. Eyed the cliff. The best place to go up was straight ahead—where there was quite possibly a rattler sleeping in the sun. To the right, the cliff jutted far out into space…but to the left, there was a narrow edge of rock that led upwards. Just a foot wide, narrowing to maybe half that for a good ten feet.

But the options…

She looked down. She fought to control her panic.

Sophie had been right. There *was* a rattler on that ledge. Huge and loosely coiled, its dusty gray diamond pattern blended perfectly with the gravel.

Below, at the bottom of the ravine, the guy had come back out of the trees. He was looking straight at her. And he very definitely had a gun.

"We've got to go, sweetheart!" Beth grabbed her hand and sidestepped along the rock, trying to calm her racing heart.

Praying that, above them, there'd be a highway.

Passing traffic. And someone with the decency to stop.

Her foot slipped on loose gravel, and she teetered for a split second. Sophie screamed and tried to grab for her, nearly sending them both over the edge before Beth found her footing once more.

An eternity later they reached the top, and Beth collapsed stomach first on the wiry grass, exhausted, with Sophie at her side.

Ahead was a sea of pastureland, far as the eye could see. But twenty feet away lay the highway…a deserted black ribbon of asphalt that trailed over the undulating land to the horizon.

And there wasn't a single vehicle or ranch building in sight. Beth closed her eyes briefly against the hopelessness of their situation.

There was no way they could outrun the man following them. There was no place to hide. He'd be on them in minutes…

And then, she remembered the snake.

## CHAPTER NINETEEN

BETH SCANNED her surroundings desperately trying
to find a safe place for Sophie in case her plan failed.

The surrounding grassland seemed to go on
forever, without a hiding place in sight. She ran a
few dozen yards, looking for the man's car. Praying
that he'd left the keys in the ignition.

If he hadn't, they'd be at his mercy.

In the middle of nowhere.

Lord knew, he wasn't coming after them to say
hello. Which left her one other option.

Sophie stood clutching her doll, looking bedraggled and exhausted. "Can we go home, Momma?"

"Soon. We'll be home soon," Beth reassured her.
"Now, I need you to do something, and I need you
to listen closely. See those sagebrush bushes over
there—the really tall ones? I need you to go over
there and sit behind them, out of sight. No matter
what happens, I want you to stay right there."

"But—"

"Go. *Now.*"

Sophie gave her a long and desperate look, then her shoulders slumped and she did as she was told.

Beth turned back to the cliff and eased close to the edge until she could just barely peer over. The man was struggling up the steep incline, his shirt soaked in sweat. And he was coming up way too fast.

Her heart faltered when she got her first good look at his face. Ewen Farley—Patrick's boss. And if he'd come all the way from Chicago, she had no doubt that he'd use the gun he held.

He was halfway up now. Three-fourths.

Almost…almost…

She picked up a handful of pebbles and held her breath. Closed her eyes briefly. Then watched as he reached for that final ledge and started to haul himself up onto it.

She dropped the pebbles and watched them ricochet crazily when they hit the ledge.

He looked up at her, his mouth twisted in a sneer. "You'd better be ready to talk, Lindstrom. Or you're good as dead."

But because he was looking up at her, he never saw what hit him.

The snake, irritated by the pebbles bouncing off its coils, drew back and struck so fast that Beth couldn't be sure it had—until he screamed and grabbed at his face.

And then he fell backward—in slow motion— out into space.

Down and down and down. Bouncing like a rag doll off another outcropping below. He landed in a cluster of bushes partway down the cliff face, silent and still.

She rocked back on her heels, unable to take another look. Feeling faint and horrified by what she'd done.

Sickened by what might have happened if she hadn't.

Shaking despite the blistering heat of the Texas sun, she ran to Sophie, knelt and enfolded her in an embrace. "We're okay, sweetie. It's all over."

"D-did that man go home?"

"I think he did. For good." Though whether to heaven or hell, Beth didn't want to guess. "We're going to start walking back toward town. Maybe we'll find a car to use—or maybe someone will come along to help us. Then we can get Viper and Darwin, okay?"

"I'm *thirsty.*"

"Me, too. So let's go."

Waves of heat shimmered above the pungent, hot asphalt as they started down the dusty shoulder. Sophie balked, then hung back. "I'm *tired.*"

"Just a little farther…just over that next rise, okay?"

"I *can't.*"

Poor thing. She'd been through a lot, and she looked it—from the scabs and scrapes on her knees to her tearstained, dirty face. And with the hot sun and parched landscape it wouldn't take any time at all for dehydration to be a threat.

Ignoring her aching muscles, Beth picked her up and kept trudging up the hill. Where, she hoped, Ewen's car would come into view. A car with keys, and enough gas to get back to Lone Wolf.

And if that prospect failed, maybe she could find the lip of the ravine and climb down to get at her rental trailer. At the last minute, she'd tossed in a twelve-pack of Coke that was probably plenty warm by now. But at least it would be wet.

*"Momma."* Her voice urgent and frightened, Sophie wrapped her arms tight around Beth's neck. "He didn't go home. He's behind us—and he has a *gun.*"

JOEL TOSSED the stack of faxes on the front seat of his truck, climbed behind the wheel and careened out of his driveway.

One hand on the steering wheel, he called the sheriff's office, then he shoved the phone in his shirt pocket.

Beth's phone message had nearly stopped his heart.

He knew someone had rammed her car. She'd said how many miles she was out of town right then. But how far had she gotten after that? Was she racing scared up the highway toward Montana—or had someone run her off the road? And if he had, were she and Sophie hurt?

Joel had tried to call her a dozen times since then. Each time, the phone had rolled into voice mail, which just upped his anxiety more. It could be out of juice. She could be out of range.

She could be lying in a ditch somewhere, unable to answer…or she could be in the hands of her assailant. And if she was, she and Sophie might not have much time to live.

Miles of asphalt, then gravel disappeared under the wheels of his truck. Once on the highway heading north, he floored the accelerator and leaned forward, scanning the sides of the road.

Afraid he might pass her.

Afraid he might see her—with her SUV crumpled in a ditch.

Knowing it was all his fault.

He should've gone to Chicago sooner. He should have made the calls, done the legwork, pulled in the favors. Nailed the bastard before he had a chance to do any more harm. What kind of defense could Beth have against someone like Ewen Farley, who had everything to lose?

Twenty miles flew past. Fifty. At seventy-two, he slowed, watching for skid marks and tire tracks veering off the road. And then, at the top of a small rise, he caught a glint of sunshine on a windshield maybe a mile ahead.

A car, parked at a crazy angle, half off the road.

Even from here, he could see the arc of black skid marks where another vehicle had veered off the road. He swallowed hard. Slamming on the brakes at a high rate of speed could've done that—and the SUV wasn't in sight.

The road dropped down into a creek bed, wound through some trees, then climbed back up. He slowed, then pulled off the road just before the top of the second rise. Grabbing flexible plastic hand-cuffs and a gun from his glove compartment, he rammed in a fresh clip and slipped quietly out of the truck. He ran up the hill on foot, staying on the asphalt and crouching low.

A good hundred feet ahead, a man slumped at the rear of the car, one hand braced against the trunk, but the gun he held was steady—and pointed straight at Beth and Sophie.

Beth darted a swift glance in Joel's direction, then sidestepped slowly around the car, holding Sophie so the child wouldn't see him—and keeping the man's back toward Joel, as well.

She carefully put Sophie down behind the car. "I swear to you, Ewen," she said clearly. "I have no idea where that key is. Patrick must've left it at his office. Maybe he never had it."

"Not possible." The man's voice was slurred. His gun hand wavered. "If you want to die over this, 'iss okay with me. Your fool husband did, damn him."

Joel moved into a firing stance, ready to call out—

But the man wobbled, his pale, sweaty face a mask of confusion.

"Give it up, Ewen—you need medical care or you'll die, and there's no one out here but me," Beth said, her voice low and calm. "I can help you."

He sank against the car, the motion exposing massive swelling and inflammation on the side of his face. His weapon fell out of his hand and clattered forgotten across the trunk.

And then he slid to the ground.

A LIFE FLIGHT HELICOPTER ARRIVED shortly after the sheriff. The flight nurse on board administered antivenin, then Ewen was airlifted to Austin for emergency surgery to release the swelling threatening to shut down his respiratory system.

The sheriff lingered, taking a full report, then went down into the ravine with Joel and Beth to survey the damage. His female partner stayed with the patrol car and Sophie, who'd fallen asleep in the backseat.

They found the trailer halfway down, its roof dented and back door hanging on one hinge, the contents littering the ravine.

"It looks like your friend was damn busy," Talbot said.

"Ewen swore I had something he wanted—but I never found it," Beth said forlornly, staring at the ruin of nearly everything she owned. An overwhelming feeling of exhaustion washed through her. "He said…he would kill me if I didn't give it to him."

"Apparently he didn't find it." Joel picked up a few books and stacked them at the back of the trailer. "We'll get a wrecker out here today, and pay the guys to clean this up. Your SUV…"

"Totaled. It rolled a few times and ended up under some trees. My dog and cat are still there— I hope."

The sheriff made his way down toward the vehicle, while Joel stayed and gently rested his hands on Beth's shoulders. He studied her face, frowning at the cut above her temple, then drew her into an embrace. "It's just incredible that you survived this." He brushed a kiss against her hair.

"Walt said you'd left to discuss a job offer," she said. "A-are you taking it?"

"I went back to turn in my resignation and clear out my things. Then I flew to Chicago, and did some research. When I found out about Ewen—"

She drew in a sharp breath. "You *knew* about him?"

"Not that he was here. I called in a few favors, and discovered that an embezzlement investigation was pointing at Ewen. A few days ago, they found evidence that he ensnared your husband in some sort of phony gambling setup—just dragged him in, deeper and deeper, to ensure his silence. Ewen disappeared after he was fired, though, and no one up there has seen him since."

"He was here in Texas," she breathed. "Probably all that time, just waiting."

"I called Talbot and took the first plane home when I heard Ewen was missing, but I wasn't nearly fast enough."

"Can you imagine how desperate Pat must have been?" Beth felt a deep wave of sadness. "He was never the type who'd take chances."

Joel nodded. "If Ewen survives, he'll have a lot of questions to answer."

"And in the meantime…" She looked at the wreckage of boxes, the clothes and household goods scattered everywhere. "I don't even know where to begin. My car…my things…"

"Not a problem. You and Sophie can come home with me. We'll have everything brought there, so you can salvage what you want."

The sheriff came up the ravine, his face glistening with sweat. He held a cat carrier in one hand and Viper's leash in the other. Straining at the leash, the dog jumped into Beth's arms as soon as she was close enough. "Beth is right. That vehicle is totaled. You folks ready to go?"

At the top of the hill, Talbot turned and held out a scrap of paper, his expression wry. "I found this on the front seat. Someone must've been trying to watch out for you."

Beth accepted the paper. It was the one she'd found in her car before leaving this morning, but she'd just tossed it aside. She opened it slowly and tried to decipher the childish, heavy scrawl.

*Somebody is watching you. Be careful.*

She thought of the man she'd seen in the shadows last night...and the way he'd once lurked across the street, then hurried away. Had Hubie been trying to protect her all this time?

"Guess it's my guardian angel," she said softly. "And I think I owe him an apology."

# CHAPTER TWENTY

BETH TAPED UP another box and set it on the stack, thankful for Joel's covered porch. A cool early morning breeze rustled through the oaks outside and sent a gentle rush of air through the screens.

It felt like heaven after yesterday—a day that had been pure hell.

After going with Sophie to the community hospital in Horseshoe Falls to be checked over, they'd both been released. Following a long discussion with the sheriff, she'd taken Sophie back to Joel's place, where Sophie had been overtired and too upset to sleep.

Beth had finally let Sophie sleep in with her, but even then, Sophie had tossed and turned, and had awakened several times, screaming.

Yesterday evening a wrecker had hauled Beth's SUV to a junkyard and the trailer here, so she could sort through her possessions, but she'd been too exhausted to even think about that task.

"Five boxes down, and eight to go," she said

wearily. "Though most of this is beyond saving. My dishes…glassware…most of it broke in the accident."

"Or when your old friend tore into everything." Joel looked up from a box of cookware.

"Ewen was never a friend." Beth shivered. "Speaking of Ewen, have you heard how he's doing?"

"The hospital refused to say. The sheriff tells me he's going to pull through, but he'll probably face a number of surgeries. There was tremendous swelling and tissue damage."

"So he probably hasn't been able to talk."

"Nope—he was unconscious most of the night. Those diamondback rattlers are nothing to mess with, and he got hit in a bad place."

Beth shook the dust out of a peach linen tablecloth and folded it. "Despite everything, I feel guilty about that. I could've warned him…."

"If you'd warned him, you and Sophie would probably be dead. Never think that you did the wrong thing." Joel set aside the box he'd just repacked and came across the room to enfold her in an embrace. "You were totally isolated, yet you protected your daughter and yourself despite not having a single weapon. That's amazing, in my book."

She leaned her forehead against his chest. She could smell his familiar scents of Dial soap and

Stetson aftershave; scents that she would forever associate with this summer, and with the man she'd come to love. A man she would soon be leaving behind. "I wish I had more answers. Even if he receives jail time for this, it won't be for long. And then will he come after me again? What could be so important, that he'd risk everything to get it?"

She felt so warm and protected in Joel's arms that it was hard to step away. She took a deep breath and tipped her head toward the piles of clothing, books and household goods still on the floor. "Guess I'd better get busy, so I can leave as soon as I have another vehicle."

"Of course." He released her with an easy, impersonal smile. "Talked to your insurance guy, have you?"

She bent down to pick up two of the antique decorative coffee tins, which were badly dented in the accident. Worthless now, except for the sentimental value, because Patrick had bought her four of them at an estate sale just after their wedding. Not long before his death, he'd joked about how they'd be worth a mint when she was old, and that she should never, ever sell them.

She wrapped each one in tissue and packed them, then searched for the other two. "The branch office in Austin is sending an adjuster down today. From what I understand, they'll be giving me a check in a few days at the most."

"I suppose you're eager to leave."

Was that a note of regret in his voice? "Not really. But I need to start my new job, and Sophie needs to be enrolled in preschool. It's time."

She found the other two coffee tins. These were older than the first two, but had survived unscathed. She wrapped one and put it into the box, then picked up the other. Both were still heavy with the original contents, which she'd once thought amusing. The coffee beans were certainly unusable, though, and the beans in this one must be bound together by mold and decay. There wasn't a typical castanet sound when she shook the can.

She tried twisting off the lid, but rust and corrosion had sealed the threads. "Can you open this?"

Joel tried once, then held the domed lid with an old rag and wrenched it loose. He handed it back and turned away to pack another box with Sophie's storybooks.

She lifted the lid to dispose of the moldering contents. Blinked. Then blindly backed up until a wicker chair hit her calves, and she sat.

It was heavy all right, but not with old coffee beans. It was packed tightly with a dense roll of papers. No—not just paper, it was money, wrapped around a folded envelope. The roll was so large that it didn't fall out when she turned the can upside down. *"Joel."*

"What?" He didn't turn around.

*"Look."* She tugged at the bills until several

came free, and then the rest tumbled out into her lap. "I...I can't *believe* this."

He came over then, his eyes widening at the pile of hundred-dollar bills in her lap. Twenty...thirty...fifty...

She gave him a handful, then counted her stack more carefully.

*Twelve thousand dollars.*

The sheer number made her feel dizzy, just thinking about the credit cards and other debts she could pay off, once and for all...except this was probably money that would have to be returned. "So this is what Ewen was after."

Joel handed her the rest of the bills. "Check the envelope."

She tried stashing the money back in the coffee tin, but it no longer fit, so she dropped it all into an empty shoe box. Picking up the envelope from the floor, she pulled out a single sheet of paper written in Patrick's hand. A small green safety deposit key packet was taped at the bottom of the letter.

She felt her eyes burn as she started to read.

Sweetheart, this is our money. I cashed out our savings, knowing we might need to leave town fast. I never meant to let things happen this way—I hope you'll forgive me someday. I made mistakes, and could never make them right—Ewen made sure of that.

I plan to tell Roger and the police everything, but if you're reading this, something bad happened first. Take this key to our old bank. With love always, Patrick.

SOPHIE SLEPT UNTIL almost eleven, then woke up with a fever and a sore throat, too ill and exhausted to travel. Every waking moment, she clung to Beth's side, still shaken by the trauma of the day before.

So when Joel offered to fly up to Chicago with the key, Beth gratefully accepted and tried to pay for his ticket. He kissed her lightly on the cheek and refused.

He returned the next evening, after meeting with investigators in the white-collar crime division of the police department in Beth's old suburb.

Beth met him at the front door of his house, one hand at her mouth. "D-did it go okay?"

Joel looked down at her and smiled. "Better than that. Before I left, an investigator had already followed the paper trail far enough to find the accounts where Ewen originally stashed the money he'd filtered from the company, and then to the accounts where he'd moved it later."

"No wonder he was in a panic to find the key to Patrick's safety deposit box."

"My guess is that Pat threatened to reveal the evidence, thinking it would make Ewen back off…but instead, it drove him to murder."

"But why, if he didn't have the key yet?"

"He probably panicked, and thought no one would ever think twice if they found some old key, anyway. Then he probably had second thoughts later, and really wanted to tie up every loose end by getting it back. We'll know more when he's well enough for more questioning."

She swallowed hard. "And what about Patrick? The accident?"

"They think Ewen ensnared him, then frightened him into complicity. Ewen already admitted forcing your car off the road on the night Patrick died."

"The same thing he did to Sophie and me…and all because of sheer, stupid greed." She sagged against the door frame as an overwhelming sense of loss rushed through her, followed by bone-deep sadness over all she'd lost because of one evil man. Her husband. Her home. The comfortable, safe life she'd always taken for granted. "At least I won't need to look over my shoulder anymore."

He searched her face. "Are you still planning to leave?"

She saw no warmth in his eyes. Nothing in his expression that made her feel as if he wanted her to stay. Maybe they'd faced a little danger together, but nothing else had really changed. Yet, what did she expect?

And why did she suddenly feel like crying, when so much was now resolved?

"The adjuster came today. He said I should have a check in a couple days, so then I'll have enough to buy another car." She managed a weak smile. "After that…yes."

He stepped around her and dropped his duffel bag on the floor, then headed for the kitchen to draw a tall glass of water. "You do have more than just that insurance check."

"Nope. That will go back into savings, with half as the start of a college account for Sophie." She rested a hand on the refrigerator. "Are you hungry? I could grill you a hamburger, or something."

He shook his head. "On my way home from the airport I stopped at Walt's place."

"For dinner?"

"More of a meeting, really…but there was food. And actually, I need to go back. Want to come along?"

"To Walt's?"

"Sort of."

Beth hesitated, remembering the sad farewells she'd already made, to people she already missed, but the thought of being alone tonight made the decision easy. "We'll go."

"Great." He lifted his glass in a vague salute toward town. "Unless Sophie's already asleep."

"Nope—she's in the den with Viper and Darwin. They've been following her like shadows after being locked in the Bravada for such a long time." She started for the den, then turned back. "Speaking of shadows, I did borrow your car for a quick trip into town this morning. I ran into Hubie."

"He's back?"

"He actually talked to me this time, though he's sure wary. He said he'd promised Crystal that he'd always look after her place when she was gone."

"And she meant…" Joel shook his head slowly.

"Just when she was away, but I think he's made it his lifelong mission, even though she'll never come back. I was afraid he was my stalker. Instead, he was trying to be my guardian."

"He probably helped keep Ewen away, too."

"No doubt." She sighed. "It's sad, thinking about Hubie, all alone. People in town think he's lurking around looking for trouble, but all he ever wanted to do was help his best friend—even after her death."

JOEL DROVE SLOWLY through town, dreading the moment when they reached their destination. Dreading what might happen. So much depended on the next fifteen minutes—he felt as if his life had been hanging in the balance for years, just waiting for this point in time when the stars aligned and everything fell into place.

Or it didn't, and he ended up with absolutely nothing.

Except Earl. Although the hound hadn't been much company over the last few weeks, since he was still missing Viper.

Beth leaned forward and peered out the windshield, then frowned. "I thought we were going to Walt's."

"Not exactly."

"Then where?" When he turned up the street to the clinic, she sat back. "The clinic, then."

He let her think that until he passed the turnoff for the clinic and pulled to a stop in front of Crystal's Café. The sun had set and shadows were lengthening across the front yard, but inside the lights were blazing both upstairs and down.

Now Beth's eyebrows drew together and she gave him a suspicious look. "You wanted me to meet the buyers?"

He offhandedly shrugged and got out of the truck, rounded the front bumper and first helped Sophie climb out, then opened Beth's door and offered her his hand.

She accepted after a moment's hesitation. "This isn't like, a party, is it? If it is, I sure didn't dress up."

The porch lights of the café highlighted the gold-and-ruby strands in her curly hair and cast shadows that accented her lovely, delicate face. Even dressed simply in khaki slacks and a dark green blouse, she was the prettiest woman he'd ever seen.

"I don't think that matters," he said. "But before we go in, I want you to know this was Walt and Loraine's idea."

"Ah. So they invited me. Not you?" She shot a teasing glance at him. "Good to know."

He'd worked undercover, dealing with the worst of the drug element. He'd investigated serial killers and had tracked down cold-blooded murderers. But never had his nerves been as unsettled as this—when he reached for the front door and ushered Beth and Sophie inside.

A cheer arose from people who filled every table, the lunch counter, and who were standing two-deep across the back.

Gina and Anna rushed forward and hugged Beth and Sophie. And then Walt and Loraine did, too, as everyone laughed and applauded.

Beth looked stunned. "I—don't understand."

Loraine steered her over to a chair and made her sit down. "We're all just grateful that you're okay—and we wanted you to know how much we care."

"And, we wanted you to know that you might be making a big mistake," added Anna, who had picked up Sophie. "Just in case you didn't know."

Gina nodded. "Walt talked to me weeks ago, and pointed out what needed to change. Only trouble was, we had trouble making it happen in time—and then all of a sudden, you were rarin' to head north."

"Thought we'd have to go up there and fetch you back, except..." Walt's eyes flashed fire. "Except for that bastard who ran you off the road and slowed you down."

Walt's housekeeper nodded vigorously. "Everyone was worried about you, you know. Trying to watch out—trying to see who could be causing you trouble. We did find out part of it—" She flicked a glance at Walt, who shook his head. "But not everything."

"Walt figured the town needed this place—and you—so he'd just better buy it before someone else did." Loraine looped her arm in Walt's. "The only thing is, we need you to stay. This place needs a good manager, you know. Someone with a real flair."

"I—" Beth looked from Walt to Loraine, her eyes filled with anguish. "I just can't."

"But what if you had good benefits, as an employee? I've got a good plan through the clinic," Walt said. "Or if you'd prefer a lease, that's fine, too."

"And we all know that you've been worried about Sophie, so when I advertised for some new teachers for this fall, I specified experience in working with hearing-impaired kids." Gina smiled triumphantly. "We've now got a dandy lined up, so we'll be ready if Sophie still needs any extra help."

Joel held his breath, hoping she'd say yes. When she lifted her gaze to his, shook her head slightly and swiftly looked away, he knew what he had to do before it was too late.

"Let's give her a few minutes, okay?" Joel nodded toward the lunch counter. "Have a cup of coffee or a beer—on the house."

He waited until conversation started humming, then turned to Beth and offered his hand once more. "Come," he said softly, hoping she wouldn't refuse. "Let's go out on the porch for a minute."

Once they were outside, he shut the door behind them. "Walt wanted it to be a surprise."

"It sure was, but I just don't know what to say." She avoided his eyes. "Everything is set. A good job. An offer on a house. There's a new life waiting for me up in Billings, and a chance to start over, away from…"

"Your problems? Maria didn't want say it in front of the crowd, but the sheriff found out that it was those wild teenage boys who trashed your yard a while back."

"Why on earth did they do it?"

"A stupid dare—nothing more than that. It's hard to believe they went to that much work."

"There were some bad rumors about poor sanitation at my café, at first—was that them as well?"

"No idea. Something like that is awfully hard to trace." Joel cleared his throat. "Talbot says you can press charges against the boys, and you could also bring a lawsuit against them, if you want. Either way, the families are all well-aware of the consequences they're facing, and you won't have any more trouble."

She waved off the suggestion. "I'm just glad it's all over."

The finality in her voice sounded like a death knell to his dreams. "I…want you to stay, Beth."

"Your uncle can find someone to run this place. He'll do fine."

"No." He rested his hands on her shoulders, and gently turned her around so she *had* to look at him. "If you leave, this town won't be the same. I won't be. Hell, Earl will probably go into a deep depression and never surface."

Her wary expression lightened. "Now, how could you ever tell if that dog looked depressed?"

"ESP. But back to me," he continued, brushing a featherlight kiss against her temple. "I need you, Beth. All the way to Chicago and back, the only thing I could think about was what it would be like if you walked out of my life."

She searched his face as if trying to find the truth. "You once said that you never want to be involved again. That you never wanted kids."

"I didn't think I could ever again stand the pain of losing someone I loved. And a child..." He swallowed hard. "But when I saw you facing Ewen, with Sophie at your side, I discovered what would be worse."

She reached up and touched his face. "Which was?"

"That if I didn't get to spend the rest of my life with you, it would break my heart. And that nothing could make me happier than learning to be the best dad I could be, for Sophie."

Beth's eyes glistened. "You really mean that."

"With all my heart. Marry me, Beth."

She laughed. "You'd go that far to keep this café running?"

This time, he didn't go for feather kisses and gentleness—he went straight to desire, kissing her long and hard and deep, until she was kissing him back exactly the same way.

When he drew back, she looked up at him, and he had no doubt that she'd say yes—and knew that he'd just made the best decision of his entire life.

And just to seal it for good, he kissed her again.

"Forever?" she murmured when they finally came up for air.

"And always." Dazed, he lifted his gaze and discovered that the faces of at least half the population of Lone Wolf were plastered against the front windows of the café—including Sophie's.

And every one of them was smiling.

Welcome to our newest miniseries, about five
poker players and the women who love them!

# Texas Hold'em

When it comes to love, the stakes are high

*Beginning October 2007 with*

# THE BABY GAMBLE

*by* USA TODAY *bestselling author*

## *Tara Taylor Quinn*

### #1446

Desperate to have a baby, Annie Kincaid
turns to the only man she trusts, her ex-husband,
Blake Smith, and asks him to father her child.

*Also watch for:*

BETTING ON SANTA *by Debra Salonen* November 2007
GOING FOR BROKE *by Linda Style* December 2007
DEAL ME IN *by Cynthia Thomason* January 2008
TEXAS BLUFF *by Linda Warren* February 2008

*Look for* THE BABY GAMBLE *by* USA TODAY
*bestselling author Tara Taylor Quinn.*

*Available October 2007 wherever you buy books.*

Ria Sterling has the gift—or is it a curse?—
of seeing a person's future in his or her
photograph. Unfortunately, when detective
Carrick Jones brings her a missing person's
case, she glimpses his partner's ID—and
sees imminent murder. And when her vision
comes true, Ria becomes the prime suspect.
Carrick isn't convinced this beautiful woman
committed the crime...but does he believe
she has the special powers to solve it?

Look for

# Seeing Is Believing

by

## Kate Austin

Available October
wherever you buy books.

# REQUEST YOUR FREE BOOKS!
## 2 FREE NOVELS PLUS 2 FREE GIFTS!

HARLEQUIN®

*Super Romance*®

### Exciting, emotional, unexpected!

**YES!** Please send me 2 FREE Harlequin Superromance® novels and my 2 FREE gifts. After receiving them, if I don't wish to receive any more books, I can return the shipping statement marked "cancel." If I don't cancel, I will receive 6 brand-new novels every month and be billed just $4.69 per book in the U.S., or $5.24 per book in Canada, plus 25¢ shipping and handling per book and applicable taxes, if any*. That's a savings of close to 15% off the cover price! I understand that accepting the 2 free books and gifts places me under no obligation to buy anything. I can always return a shipment and cancel at any time. Even if I never buy another book from Harlequin, the two free books and gifts are mine to keep forever.

135 HDN EEX7   336 HDN EEYK

| Name | (PLEASE PRINT) | |
|---|---|---|
| Address | | Apt. |
| City | State/Prov. | Zip/Postal Code |

Signature (if under 18, a parent or guardian must sign)

Mail to the **Harlequin Reader Service**®:

**IN U.S.A.:** P.O. Box 1867, Buffalo, NY 14240-1867
**IN CANADA:** P.O. Box 609, Fort Erie, Ontario L2A 5X3

Not valid to current Harlequin Superromance subscribers.

### Want to try two free books from another line?
### Call 1-800-873-8635 or visit www.morefreebooks.com.

* Terms and prices subject to change without notice. NY residents add applicable sales tax. Canadian residents will be charged applicable provincial taxes and GST. This offer is limited to one order per household. All orders subject to approval. Credit or debit balances in a customer's account(s) may be offset by any other outstanding balance owed by or to the customer. Please allow 4 to 6 weeks for delivery.

**Your Privacy:** Harlequin is committed to protecting your privacy. Our Privacy Policy is available online at www.eHarlequin.com or upon request from the Reader Service. From time to time we make our lists of customers available to reputable firms who may have a product or service of interest to you. If you would prefer we not share your name and address, please check here. ☐

HSR07

*74 Seaside Avenue*

### *New York Times* Bestselling Author

# DEBBIE MACOMBER

Dear Reader:

I'm living a life I couldn't even have dreamed of a few years ago. I'm married to Bobby Polgar now, and we've got this beautiful house with a view of Puget Sound.

Lately something's been worrying Bobby, though. When I asked, he said he was "protecting his queen"—and I got the oddest feeling he wasn't talking about chess but about me. He wouldn't say anything else.

Do you remember Get Nailed, the beauty salon in Cedar Cove? I still work there. I'll tell you about my friend Rachel, and I'll let you in on what I've heard about Linnette McAfee. Come in soon for a manicure and a chat, okay?

*Teri (Miller) Polgar*

"Those who enjoy good-spirited,
gossipy writing will be hooked."
—*Publishers Weekly* on *6 Rainier Drive*

*Available the first week of September 2007,
wherever paperbacks are sold!*
**www.MIRABooks.com**

MIRA®

# ATHENA FORCE

*Heart-pounding romance and thrilling adventure.*

## A deadly masquerade

As an undercover asset for the FBI, mafia princess Sasha Bracciali can deceive and improvise at a moment's notice. But when she's cut off from everything she knows, including her FBI-agent lover, Sasha realizes her deceptions have masked a painful truth: she doesn't know whom to trust. If she doesn't figure it out quickly, her most ambitious charade will also be her last.

Look for

# CHARADE
by *Kate Donovan*

*Available in October wherever you buy books.*

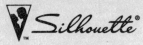

## Romantic
# SUSPENSE

### Sparked by Danger, Fueled by Passion.

When evidence is found that Mallory Dawes intends to sell the personal financial information of government employees to "the Russian," OMEGA engages undercover agent Cutter Smith. Tailing her all the way to France, Cutter is fighting a growing attraction to Mallory while at the same time having to determine her connection to "the Russian." Is Mallory really the mouse in this game of cat and mouse?

### Look for

# *Stranded with a Spy*

### by *USA TODAY* bestselling author

# Merline Lovelace

### *October 2007.*

Also available October wherever you buy books:

BULLETPROOF MARRIAGE *(Mission: Impassioned)*
by Karen Whiddon

A HERO'S REDEMPTION *(Haven)* by Suzanne McMinn

TOUCHED BY FIRE by Elizabeth Sinclair

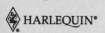

# EVERLASTING LOVE™

*Every great love has a story to tell™*

*An uplifting story of love and survival that spans generations.*

Hayden MacNulty and Brian Conway both lived on Briar Hill Road their whole lives. As children they were destined to meet, but as a couple Hayden and Brian have much to overcome before romance ultimately flourishes.

**Look for**

## The House on Briar Hill Road

**by award-winning author**
## Holly Jacobs

**Available October wherever you buy books.**

# COMING NEXT MONTH

### #1446 THE BABY GAMBLE • Tara Taylor Quinn
*Texas Hold 'Em*
Desperate to have a baby, Annie Kincaid turns to the only man she trusts—her ex-husband, Blake Smith—and asks him to father her child. Because when it comes to love, the stakes are high....

### #1447 TEMPORARY NANNY • Carrie Weaver
Who would guess that the perfect nanny for a ten-year-old boy is Royce McIntyre? Not Katy Garner, that's for sure. But she has no other choice than to ask her handsome neighbor for help. Never expecting that Royce might be the perfect answer for someone else...

### #1448 COUNT ON LOVE • Melinda Curtis
*Going Back*
Annie Raye's a single mom who's trying to rebuild her life after her ex-husband, a convict, tarnished her reputation. But returning home to Las Vegas makes "going straight" difficult because she's still remembered as a child gambling prodigy. And it doesn't help when Sam Knight costs her a good job. So she sets out to prove the private investigator wrong.

### #1449 BECAUSE OF A BOY • Anna DeStefano
*Atlanta Heroes*
Nurse Kate Rhodes mistakenly believes one of her young charges is being abused by his dad and sets in motion a series of events that jeopardize the lives of the young boy and his father, who are forced to go into hiding. To right her wrong, she must work with Stephen Creighton, the legal advocate who's defending the accused father, and find the pair before it's too late.

### #1450 THE BABY DOCTORS • Janice Macdonald
When widowed pediatrician Sarah Benedict returns home after fifteen years in Central America, she wants to set up a practice where traditional and alternative medicine work together. And she hopes to team up with Matthew Cameron, the friend she's loved since she was eight. Loved *and* lost, when he married someone else. Except now he's divorced...and she doesn't like the person he's become.

### #1451 WHERE LOVE GROWS • Cynthia Reese
Becca Reynolds has a job to do—investigate the suspicious insurance claims of several farmers. Little does she realize that she "knows" one of the men in question. Could Ryan MacIntosh really be involved? And will she be able to find out before he figures out who she is?